W9-ART-674

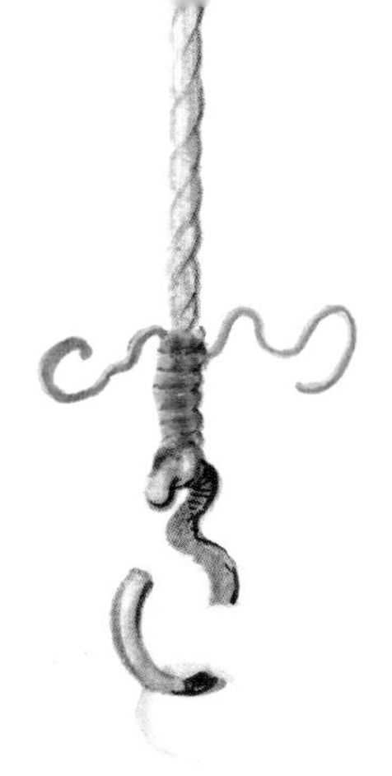

Advice comes in many shapes. Poems come in many shapes. And so, it follows, poems of advice come in many shapes too.

Sometimes they look you in the eye and say, “Do this! Don’t do that!”

Sometimes they sidle up beside you and whisper, “Have you ever thought about . . . ?”

And sometimes they don’t seem to make any sense at all, and just seem to be going on about jelly for some reason.

Quack, quack, quack.

Also by A. F. Harrold

The Afterwards
Illustrated by Emily Gravett

The Imaginary
Illustrated by Emily Gravett

The Song from Somewhere Else
Illustrated by Levi Pinfold

THE BOOK OF NOT ENTIRELY USEFUL ADVICE

BUM

A. F. HARROLD

illustrated by

MINI GREY

BLOOMSBURY
CHILDREN'S BOOKS
NEW YORK LONDON OXFORD NEW DELHI SYDNEY

BLOOMSBURY CHILDREN'S BOOKS
Bloomsbury Publishing Inc., part of Bloomsbury Publishing Plc
1385 Broadway, New York, NY 10018

BLOOMSBURY, BLOOMSBURY CHILDREN'S BOOKS, and the Diana logo
are trademarks of Bloomsbury Publishing Plc

First published in Great Britain in September 2020 by Bloomsbury Publishing Plc
Published in the United States of America in March 2021
by Bloomsbury Children's Books

Library of Congress Cataloging-in-Publication Data
Names: Harrold, A. F. | Grey, Mini, illustrator.
Title: The book of not entirely useful advice / by A. F. Harrold ; illustrated by Mini Grey.
Description: New York : Bloomsbury, 2021.
Summary: Packed with silly rhymes and witty wordplay, A. F. Harrold's poetry is positively bursting
with fun and advice. But it's not always the most useful . . .
Identifiers: LCCN 2020029207 (print) | LCCN 2020029208 (e-book)
ISBN 978-1-5476-0677-1 (hardcover)
ISBN 978-1-5476-0678-8 (e-book) • ISBN 978-1-5476-0679-5 (e-PDF)
Subjects: LCSH: Children's poetry, English. | Humorous poetry, English.
Classification: LCC PR6108.A786 B66 2021 (print) | LCC PR6108.A786 (e-book) | DDC 811/.54—dc23
LC record available at https://lccn.loc.gov/2020029207
LC e-book record available at https://lccn.loc.gov/2020029208

Book design by Jeni Child
Typeset in Trocchi
Printed in China by C&C Offset Printing Co., Ltd., Shenzhen, Guangdong
2 4 6 8 10 9 7 5 3 1

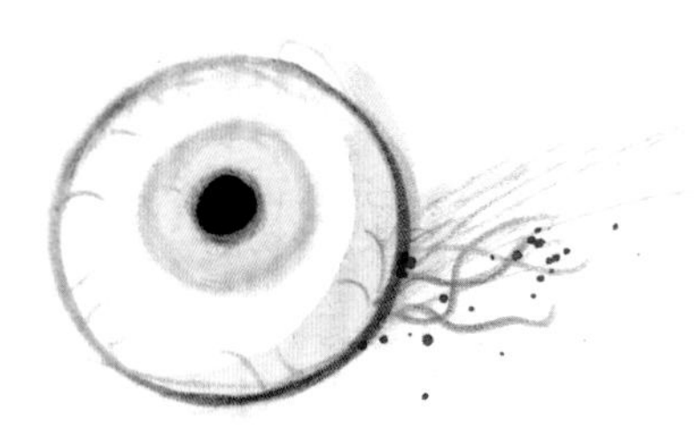

For Roger and Brian
(McGough and Patten, respectively),
this is all your fault
–A. F. H.

For John Vernon Lord
with vindaloo and rice
–love from Mini

Contents

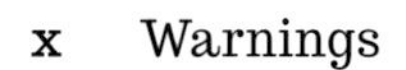

x Warnings
xi A Note for the Reader

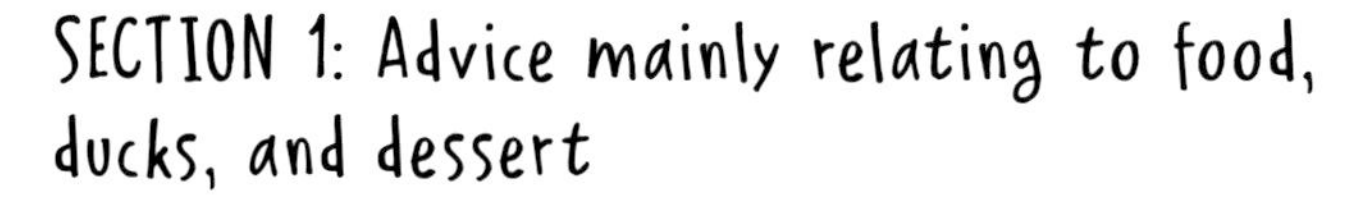

SECTION 1: Advice mainly relating to food, ducks, and dessert

3 The Perils of Breakfast
4 Breakfast Is Not Boring
7 The Most Toast
8 Advert
9 The Secret Life of the Cabbage
10 Duck Soup
11 Cat Soup
12 Useful
14 Gravy Is Not Perfume
15 The New Farmer Learns
16 Some Home Truths
17 Rock Cakes
18 Blackbirds and Bananas
19 Burger Tips
20 How Many Is Too Many?
20 Roots
22 A Restaurant to Avoid
24 Dunk
26 Granny's Biscuits from the Back of the Cupboard
28 Tea

29 The Dangers of Rock and Roll
30 Pudding Song
32 An Exercise in Taste
33 Jelly Is Never Wrong
34 Dangerous Habits
36 Further Notes for the Reader

SECTION 2: Advice mainly relating to animals, giants, and the natural world

42 Juggles
43 Kissing Advice
45 Parrots Are Not to Be Confused with Dogs
46 Smaller Ones Are Better
48 Rabbit Risks
49 Nasty Rabbit Poem
50 Playing with Pets
51 Burying the Dog
52 *Vulpes vulpes*
53 The Hedgehog
55 The Kilted Koala
57 How to Avoid a Giant Who Has Escaped from a Nearby Fairy Tale
58 The Ambitious Spider
60 Inside the Anthill
61 Grow Your Own
62 Holiday
63 Earth Song
64 More Further Notes for the Reader
65 The Advice-a-Tron 216

we like
fish

Sometimes if you want something to exist you have to make it yourself.

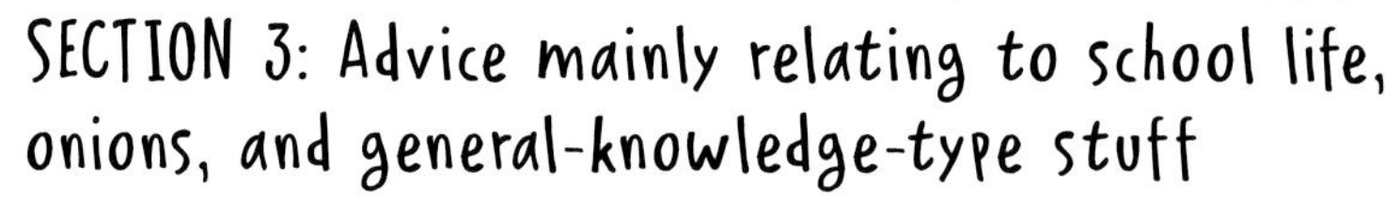

SECTION 3: Advice mainly relating to school life, onions, and general-knowledge-type stuff

Follow
a
duck.

68 The Value of an Onion
70 The Problem of the Wrong Oblong
71 The Day I Ate My Pencil
72 Inside
73 Dear Diary
74 Belt Advice
76 Eagles and Elephants
77 Testing Hats
78 Zombie Monitor
79 Quiet
80 Moon
81 Alonely
83 Wednesday's the High Point of the Week
85 All at Sea
86 Even More Further Notes for the Reader

SECTION 4: Advice mainly relating to the human condition, dreams, and miscellaneous other subjects that didn't fit elsewhere

91 Expectations
92 Crosses
93 Knot Knots
94 In the Dark
96 Clouds

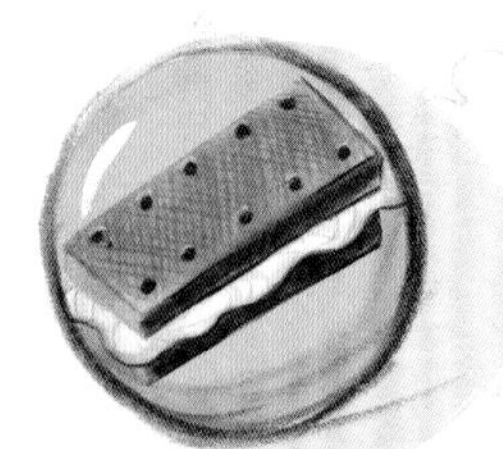

Time for
Tea

ROCK
or CAKE?

97 Dreamless
98 The Idea of It
99 Advice for the Nervous
100 Bin
102 Silences
103 Sing a Happy Song
104 Poet at the Disco
105 Numb and Number
106 Useless
107 The Poet Gives Some Free Advice
108 Butler
109 The Exaggerator
110 Two Quick Tips
112 Say Something Nice
114 Bath Poem
115 Umbrella Poem
116 Jumper
117 Expedition to the Heart of the Jumble Sale
118 The Point
119 Winch
120 Perils of the Bouncy Castle
121 Missing
122 Some Final Further Notes for the Reader

124 Final Notes for the Reader Wishing to Continue Their Adventure in Advice
126 Index of Advice, Examples, Morals, and Useful Lessons
145 Acknowledgments
146 Biographies

WHY NOT?

Warnings

Don't do that.
Or that.
Or that.

As cute as it looks.
As bright as a button.
As sweet as honey pie.

It might shock you.
It might bite you.
It might smile wickedly when you turn away.

So just don't.
Don't.
Don't say I didn't warn you.

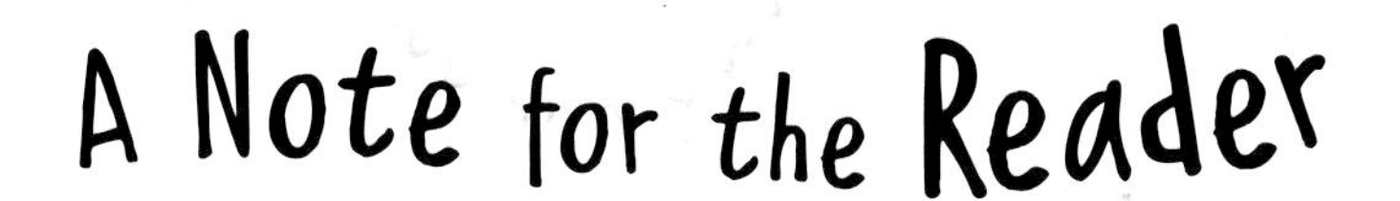

It's a dangerous world, and so I have created this book to keep readers everywhere safe.

I've filled it with all the advice I could think of. Everything I've learned over this long, long life of mine, and I believe the poems in this book will not only make you happy, not only keep you safe, but also—most importantly—stop you from getting eaten by tigers.

My friend Mini (who also knows all sorts of useful things and has never been eaten by a tiger) has made the pictures for this book, so that even people who don't usually like poems will be able to learn ways to survive this tricky and treacherous world, just by looking at the beautifully colorful advice-filled pages.

All you have to do, as the reader of these poems and advice, is to use your brain and work out for yourself which bits to follow and which bits to ignore. It is honestly so simple that I am willing to offer a MONEY BACK GUARANTEE!

If, after you have read this book and absorbed all the advice, you still get eaten by a tiger, in Bournemouth, on a Thursday afternoon in August, while talking to a woman called Gerald Bumbersnook, then I will happily, without quibbling, refund you the entire price of this book—upon receipt of a letter from your mum, sent to me via the publisher (address in the front of this book). I can't say fairer than that, can I?

So, onward into the poems, my brave reader of wonders . . .

BOURBON
DUCK
SOUP

SECTION 1

Advice mainly relating to food, ducks, and dessert

INGREDIENTS: CORN, SUGAR, SALT, MALT,
NIACIN, THIAMIN, RIBOFLAVIN, VITAMIN A, VITAMIN B, VITAMIN Z,
IRON, RUST, SAWDUST, CARDBOARD
MAY CONTAIN TRACES OF BEAR
Spellogs
CORN FLAKES

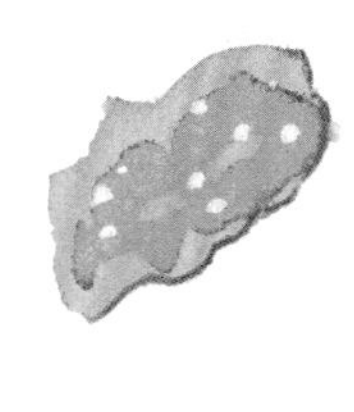

The Perils of Breakfast

Watch out for bears in your cornflakes.

Bears are dangerous.
Bears have big claws.
Bears are always hungry.
At breakfast time, doubly so.

If you lift a spoonful of cornflakes to your mouth
and it's got a bear hiding in it,
well,
you'll be in trouble then. Won't you?
Eaten up just like that.
Gobble. Gobble. *Crunch.*

Fortunately
bears are larger than cornflakes
and so you can usually spot
a little bit of fur poking round the side.

If you do
spot a little bit of fur poking round the side
of the cornflake
in the spoon
you've lifted up to your mouth to have for your breakfast
then just put your spoon down,
step away
and choose something else instead.

But
watch out for crocodiles in your porridge
and watch out for tigers under your toast.

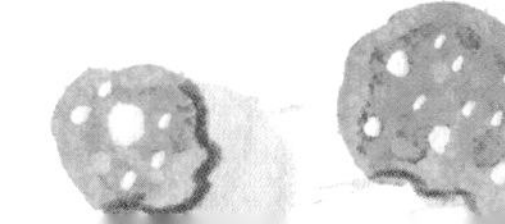

Breakfast Is Not Boring

In order
to make breakfast
more enjoyable
I pretend to be
a different animal each day.

Today I was a warthog
wallowing in my cereal bowl.

Yesterday I was a parrot
shouting
rude words
from the top of the kitchen cupboard.

Tomorrow I'll be a chameleon
and paint myself
the same color
as the chair,
with bold felt-tips.

I think
it's important to have a hobby

and,
my mum says,
a good wash
before you go to school.

BUM
Flakes

The Most Toast

For breakfast I like to have the most toast.
I'll have three slices if you have two.
If you have an extra one, I'll take another.
If the bread's run out, I'll steal it from my brother's plate.

I should have a medal for the toast I've eaten.
It'd be a winner's medal—I've never been beaten.
You can't have my medal—you've not et enough.
When the toast gets going, my teeth get tough.

I eat the most toast 'cause I want to be the best,
but I ain't no good at playing the piano,
I can't paint a seagull or write a great play
and I've never scored a goal at home or away . . .

So . . . I eat the most toast.
I eat the most toast.
I know it's a boastful thing to say
but I can eat toast, I can eat toast, I can eat toast all day.

Now, when people see me coming they all sing:
Here comes the toast-man to-oast!—which *is* embarrassing,
but true.
Eating toast is my skill. What do you do?

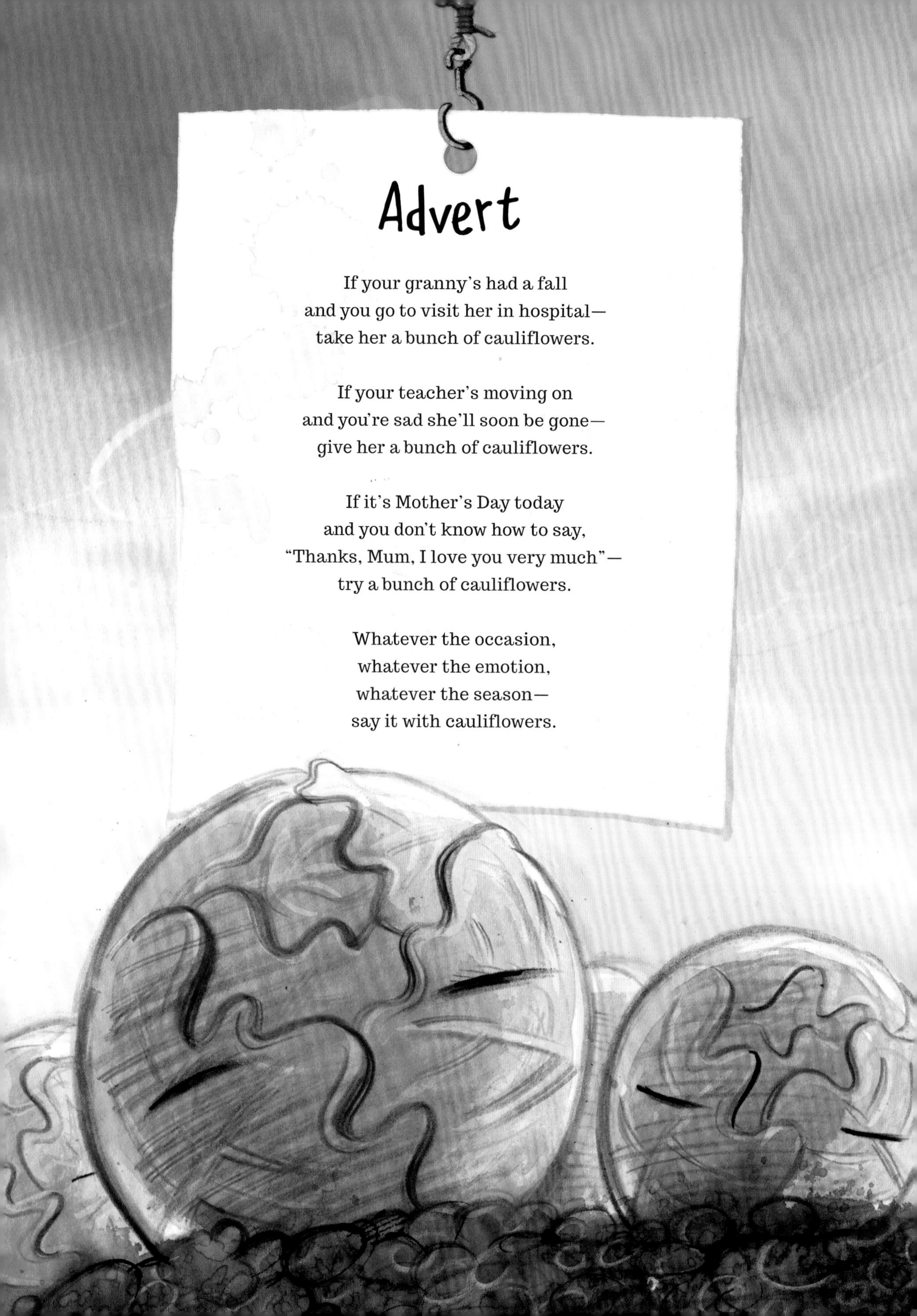

Advert

If your granny's had a fall
and you go to visit her in hospital—
take her a bunch of cauliflowers.

If your teacher's moving on
and you're sad she'll soon be gone—
give her a bunch of cauliflowers.

If it's Mother's Day today
and you don't know how to say,
"Thanks, Mum, I love you very much"—
try a bunch of cauliflowers.

Whatever the occasion,
whatever the emotion,
whatever the season—
say it with cauliflowers.

The Secret Life of the Cabbage

In the middle of the night
when the lights are out,
the cabbages . . . start rolling.

Uprooted from the earth
they tumble down the hills,
bouncing in the moonlight.

Oh! Cabbages love to roll,
cabbages love to bounce,
cabbages love to be free.

Every morning men and women
with shovels scoop them up
and clear the roads and paths.

They bed in their reaching roots,
replant them in the earth,
recabbage the decabbaged fields.

If you've never seen the cabbages
heaped up outside your house in the morning then
those men and women have done their job.

But one day, when money's tight,
and they've been made unemployed,
it'll be cabbages for breakfast and for breakfast
and for breakfast.

Duck Soup

There's a duck in my soup
and it's swimming round and round.

The soup bowl is small
but the duck doesn't mind.

It's warmer than the river
where the water's rather cold.

I've asked the duck to leave,
but this duck just won't be told.

So I dress up like a swan
and I climb in too.

And I hiss and I flap
like angry swans do.

And the duck flies off
in a quacking little huff.

And I paddle-drink-paddle
and I sip the soupy stuff . . .

which tastes like the underside
of a swimming duck,

which is weedy and muddy
and really quite horrid,

so I call the waiter over
and ask for a new bowl of soup
and he asks me why I'm dressed up like a swan
and I don't really have a good answer to that
and I'm asked to leave the restaurant
and never come back.

Cat Soup

Don't serve a cat soup when the cat wants jelly.
Tomato soup won't fill a feline belly.
Mouse-meat in jelly's what should be in the bowl—
it's the best thing to fill a cat's hunger-hole.

A cat will get angry if you serve it soup,
or sauce-filled spaghetti (Alphabetti or Hoops).
All it wants is meat, fresh off the bone.
If you can't give it meat, best to leave it alone.

Useful

Sausages can be useful
if you're ever lost at sea.

You can set fire to them
to attract aeroplanes.

You can dangle them in the water
to attract sharks.

You can balance them on your lip
and pretend to have a mustache
in order to amuse your companions.

There is no end
to the uses of sausages.

Now, here's some blank space for you
to add some uses of your own:

Very good. I like what you did there.

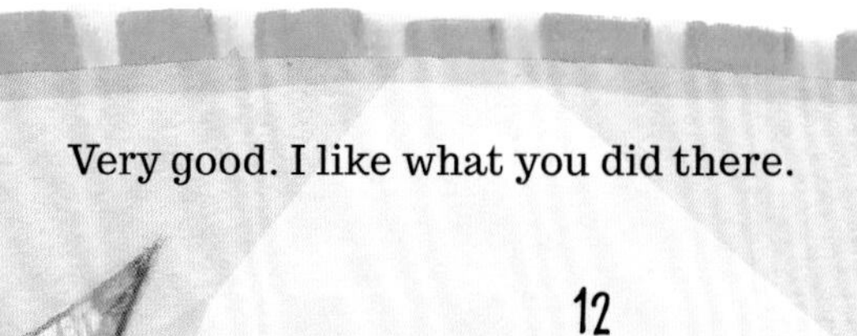

Gravy Is Not Perfume

People who dab gravy
on their wrists
and below their ears
get eaten by dogs
more often than people who don't.

So, if your mother says to do it,
be sure to say you won't.

The New Farmer Learns

I wish I'd then known then
what I now know now—
that it's eggs from the chickens
and milk from the cow.

You see, my first day was rainy,
but worse than that—
I drank chicken juice
with a soft-boiled pat.

Some Home Truths

You can't make an omelette
  without cracking some eggs.
You can't have a skiing trip
  without breaking some legs.
You can't have a washing line
  without pinching some pegs.

You can't make a cake
  without spilling some flour.
You can't make a rainbow
  without raining a shower.
You can't spread some honey
  without knowing some bees who've visited a flower
or two.

You can't have Jack Horner
  without a pie made of plum.
You can't get a good grip on things
  without opposing your thumb.
You can't have a nice sit down
  without putting a chair between the floor and your
buttocks.

A
B
C
D
E
F
G
H
I
Z
Illustrator's note:
Some items on this page are rocks, and some items are cakes. And some are rock cakes.
Can you tell which are which?
Answers up the side.

Rock Cakes

In the same way that butterflies
have pictures of eyes

on their wings
to scare off hungry things,

and people who wear camouflage trousers
don't want you to see their legs,

so do rock cakes
pretend to be rocks.

They don't want you to eat them.
The world is a complicated place.

ANSWERS: A:cake B:rock C:rock cake D:rock E:rock F:rock G:rock H:cake I:rock cake J:rock K:rock L:rock
M:cake N:rock O:rock cake P:rock Q:rock cake R:rock S:cake T:cake U:cake V:rock W:rock X:rock Y:cake Z:rock

Blackbirds and Bananas

A banana is yellow, with little bits of black.
A blackbird is black, with little bits of yellow.

A banana grows up in a tree.
A blackbird grows up in a tree.

A banana is about the size of a blackbird.
A blackbird is about the size of a banana.

A banana is a surprising, but not unheard of, pie filling.
A blackbird is a surprising, but not unheard of, pie filling.

A banana. A blackbird.
A blackbird. A banana.

Listen!
My lunch box is singing.

Burger Tips

Brown and crispy
dripping with juice
I like my burgers
made from moose,
but little bones
can make you cough
so I always saw
the antlers off.

How Many Is Too Many?

Too many cooks spoil the broth.
Too many spoons spoil the soup.

Too much sand spoils the sandwich.
And too many tigers spoil the picnic.

How many tigers is too many tigers?

Let's count them . . .

No tigers at the picnic:
perfect.

One tiger at the picnic:
too many.

Roots

It's a good picnic
to which you need carry no food,
simply slip off your shoes,
let your toes grow down,
rootling around,
deep into the soil,
supping and sifting,
and you palm up your hands
and drink
the sunshine.

A Restaurant to Avoid

Susan sips her soup.
Philip flips his fish.
Nicky nibbles her nachos.
Derek dabs his dish.

Charlie chomps on cheese.
Kevin crunches crisps.
Priya prays for pineapple.
Colin crunches crisps, too.

Billy belches big burps.
Roberta ravages rice.
Jenny jiggles jelly.
Morris munches mice.

(Note: it's possible that at least one of these people is a cat.)

Dunk

To dunk or not to dunk?
Dunk or don't dunk?

Dunk, don't dunk, or just dunk a little bit?

Is dipping the same as dunking?
Duncan dips
his toes in the tea. Did he dunk?

Diana dunks her shortbread finger
in the goldfish bowl.
Did she dip?

Dunking, dipping, dipping, dunking.

Dougie slam dunks
the basketball
in the sugar bowl.
He dunked, but didn't dip.

To dip, to dunk,
what have we learned today?

Don't invite
Duncan, Diana, or Dougie
for afternoon tea,
maybe.

Granny's Biscuits from the Back of the Cupboard

My granny makes me sit down when I go and visit her.
She kettles up some water and she gives the tea a stir.

She pours it out all hot and sweet but then it goes to pot—
the biscuits that she offers next are tasty, tasty. Not!

They're Bourbonzola, Bourbonzola—the chocolatey biscuit with the smelly-cheese inner!
Bourbonzola! Bourbonzola! Dunk 'em in your tea if you're feeling brave . . .

Of course I love my granny but she won't take the answer "No."
"You're a growing lad," she says to me, "and biscuits help you grow."

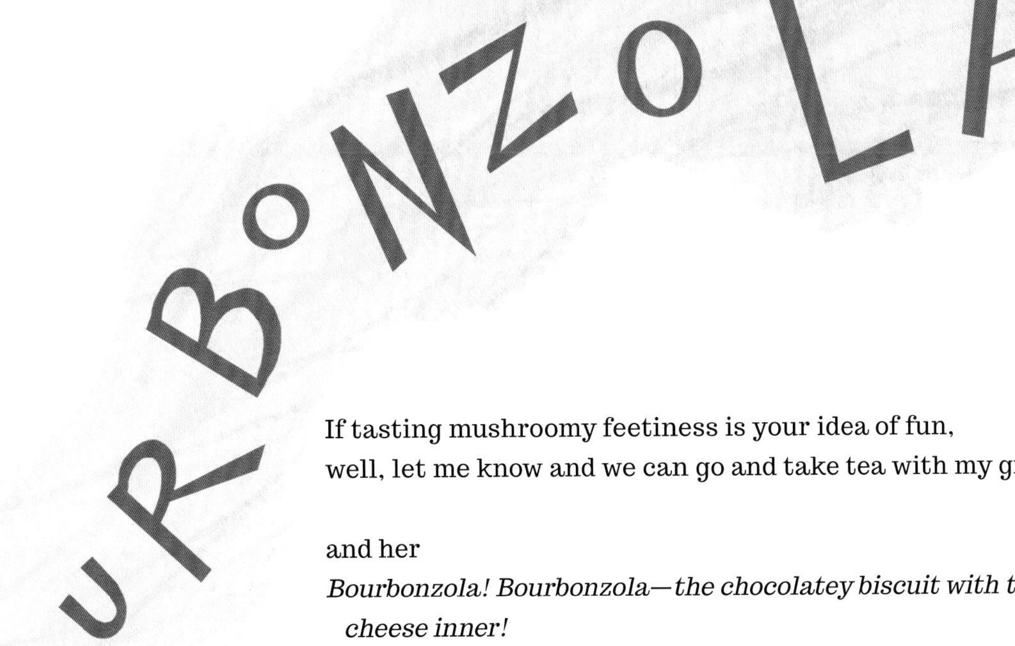

If tasting mushroomy feetiness is your idea of fun,
well, let me know and we can go and take tea with my gran,

and her
Bourbonzola! Bourbonzola—the chocolatey biscuit with the smelly-cheese inner!
Bourbonzola! Bourbonzola! Scrape up the cheesy paste to really get the tang . . .

My mum and dad cottoned on a long, long time ago.
They always get a headache, or a broken leg and so,

it's: "We'd love to visit Granny, but . . ." I'm sent off on my own.
But I'm getting my revenge today because when I get back home

I'll breathe my—
Bourbonzola breath, Bourbonzola breath, all through the house and into their faces.
Bourbonzola breath, it smells a bit like Death! (If Death kept its socks on for a year and a day . . .)
Hey!
Lean in close and I'll read you the end of the poem . . .

Bourbonzola!

Tea

Some people say
you can tell the future
from the shape of a person's used teabag.

My future is square and soggy
and full of holes.

My future is cold
and drips darkly down the side of the sink.

My future falls with a wet *thlud*
into the bin.

I think
I might stop drinking tea.

Your Future:
You may find yourself
in hot water.

The Dangers of Rock and Roll

Don't put a rock in a roll,
unless you hate having teeth.

And be careful when rolling rocks,
in case you end up underneath.

Pudding Song

Stick your pudding in your face,
chew it up and swallow well,
lick your lips and ask for more
and feel your skin begin to swell.

Pud is good!
Oh! Pud is good! (repeat chorus several times, happily)

Wood is good for making boats,
wood is good because it floats,
but bite down on a plank of wood
and you will find wood is not pud.

Pud is good!
Oh! Pud is good! (repeat chorus several times, excitedly)

Bricks are good at building houses,
denim's good at making trousers,
gold and diamonds make a ring,
but for dessert pud is the thing.

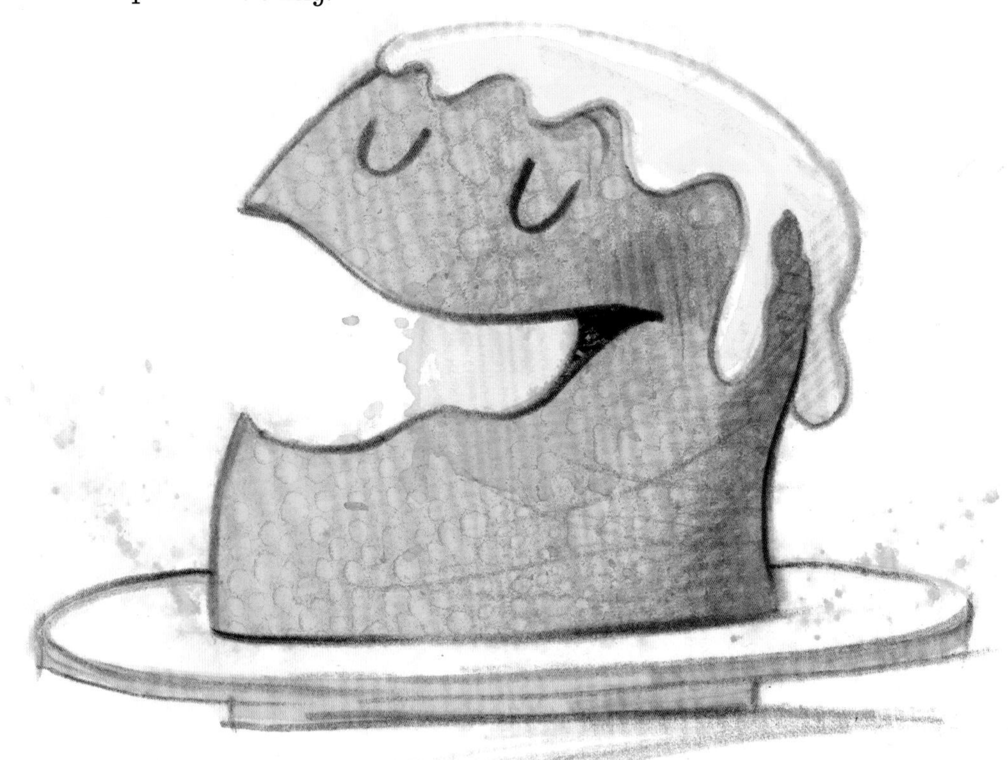

Pud is good!
Oh! Pud is good! (repeat chorus several times, in a sing-song voice)

Don't get confused and eat a book,
a porcupine or a babbling brook,
these things are good at what they do,
but none of them belong in you.

Pud is good!
Oh! Pud is good! (repeat chorus several times, solemnly, becoming more exuberant)

Yes! Pudding's good and generous
and loves you back as you love it,
but if you feel you're full to pop,
then only have a little bit.

An Exercise in Taste

I've tried helicopter
and hot-air balloon,

and I've tried albatross
and Zeppelin,

and I've tried cloud
and rainbow,

but at the end of the day,
I have to say,

for the best taste of the sky,
so fast and vast and high,

cruising sedately
with an in-flight movie . . .

it's plane crisps for me
every time.

Jelly Is Never Wrong

Raspberry flavor jelly for my birthday.
Strawberry flavor jelly for my lunch.
Cranberry flavor jelly for Christmas day.
Melon flavor jelly makes me munch.

Wobble, wobble, wobble,
gobble, gobble, gulp.

Cabbage flavor jelly for Tuesday afternoon.
Marmite flavor jelly on my toast.
Goulash flavor jelly for Halloween.
Potato flavor jelly with a roast.

Wobble, wobble, wobble,
gobble, gobble, slurp.

Pickled-onion flavor jelly just before a kiss.
Tickled-squirrel flavor jelly for a laugh.
But the king of all jellies, the one I really love,
is the jelly you find floating in the bath.

Quack, quack, quack.

Dangerous Habits

Letting the broccoli drive the car.
Keeping a porcupine in your bra.
Making a sausage out of hair.
Voting a boomerang in as mayor.
Carving a duvet out of ice.
Letting the cat babysit the mice.
Asking an opera singer to tea.
Dressing your sister up as me.
Setting three dozen socks on fire.
Calling your own left knee a liar.
Singing, "My darling, I'm so glad you're going!"
Wondering, "What is the point of this poem?"

The
RIGHT
WORSHIPFUL
LADY
BOOMERANG

Further Notes for the Reader

Here are some important bits of advice that we didn't have time to find homes for in poems:

Don't put mustard on dogs, no matter how hot they look, unless you know the dog very well beforehand.
Do not use your nose as a piggy bank, no matter how fragrant the money smells.
It's your own time you're wasting.
(Mini's note)
WAR & FLEAS what the critics said:
"Frankly unbelievable with atroshus speling"
A.F. HARROLD
M. MORPURGO
WAR & FLEAS
Fleo Trollstoy

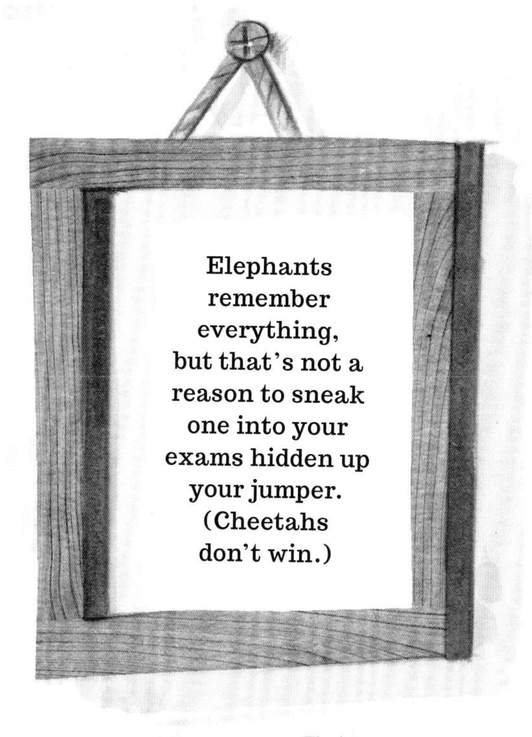
Elephants
remember
everything,
but that's not a
reason to sneak
one into your
exams hidden up
your jumper.
(Cheetahs
don't win.)

Just because
that tree is
older than you
doesn't mean
it wants a
birthday cake.

Never
apologize to
a door you've
walked into,
unless it's a
really special
door.

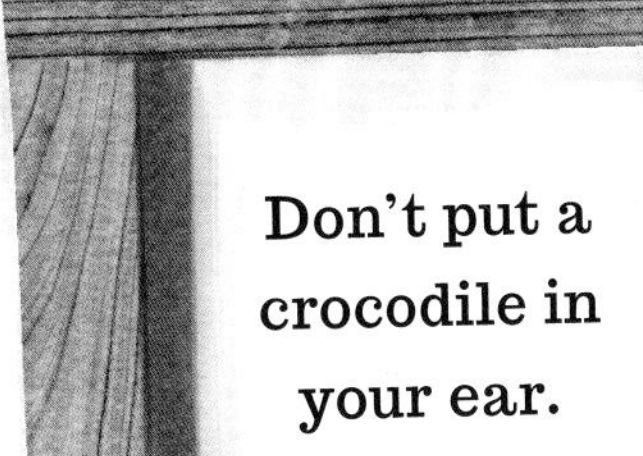
Don't put a
crocodile in
your ear.

Don't read books
by other authors.
Most of them are
crummy and are full of
spelling misatkes.

This page has been left blank for you to write your own poem or draw your own picture to bring these important morals to life.

SECTION 2

Advice mainly relating to animals, giants, and the natural world

Juggles

Don't juggle in the jungle
if your juggling's not great.

Monkeys are judgmental
and they whisper mate to mate,

saying, "Cop a lot of that chap
chucking juggles everywhere."

And they turn away, embarrassed,
showing bottoms that are bare . . .

which is, it must be said,
just the sort of thing

that distracts a trainee juggler
from their trainee juggling.

Kissing Advice

Don't kiss
anything with a hiss.

Unless you're a snake
and the hiss is your mate

saying, "Give us a kiss."
In which case: yes!

Kiss
the hiss.

(But if they're a python who wants to get cuddly,
be sure to say,
"Not today.")

BUM

TIDDLES

Parrots Are Not to Be Confused with Dogs

A few tips:

If you take a parrot for a walk
there's only one thing you'll need
and that's a very long lead
because parrots tend to fly
higher in the sky
than dogs do.

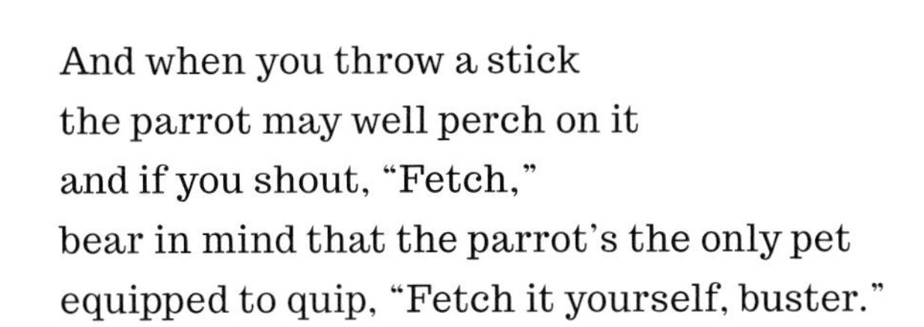

And when you throw a stick
the parrot may well perch on it
and if you shout, "Fetch,"
bear in mind that the parrot's the only pet
equipped to quip, "Fetch it yourself, buster."

Smaller Ones Are Better

Never get a pet bigger than yourself.
Oversized animals are bad for your health.

Take a snake that could swallow you whole.
A great white shark won't fit a fishbowl.

You might try to keep a polar bear in the freezer,
but don't tell your mum, 'cause the news wouldn't please her.

A bottlenose dolphin hogs the bath.
A big butch hyena is good for a laugh,

but when it gets peckish, starts looking for lunch,
the last sound you'll hear is a mighty meaty munch.

And it's the same with a tiger, the same with a lion,
don't get a walrus, and don't think of trying

to befriend a blue whale: they're bigger than buses,
and when the food bill arrives, then you'll see what a fuss is.

Don't get a pet bigger than a person,
smaller ones are better. You bet you'd start cursing

if you had to clear up all the mess that you find
fallen to the floor from an elephant's behind.

A rhinoceros might be a tough old trooper
but it tends to overwork the tired pooper scooper.

So, stick with a stick insect, stick with the cat,
befriend a little rabbit or a mouse or a rat

or a sensible dog or a gerbil or a parrot . . .
or smallest and safest . . . a crunchy tender carrot.

Rabbit Risks

The rabbit eating raisins
has to be very careful
she doesn't turn around
and carry on eating raisins.

(The reason is: the raisins
behind a rabbit aren't raisins.
(A rabbit should be stopping
when it nibbles on a dropping.))

ZOOLOGICAL NOTE
FROM THE ILLUSTRATOR:
Actually I think you'll find that
rabbits do actually
eat their droppings
as part of their normal diet -
it's a way of getting
enough nutrients.

Nasty Rabbit Poem

My rabbit's got four lucky feet:
one at each corner.

My sister tried to make him hop.
I tried to warn her.

My rabbit's shy and lazy,
with big incisor teeth.

My sister's full of holes now
and is lying underneath

the tombstone in the graveyard.
The moral runs thus:

If you go round poking rabbits,
they're gonna make a fuss.

Playing with Pets

Some kids play fetch with their dogs
and spoil them with all their love.

Some kids play catch with hedgehogs,
but they only spoil their gloves.

Burying the Dog

We buried the dog in the garden,
  where it had buried its bones.
We patted the earth down neatly
  and piled up some stones.

When mum saw what we'd done,
  she made us dig him up quick.
He was only asleep when we buried him,
  but now he's looking quite sick.

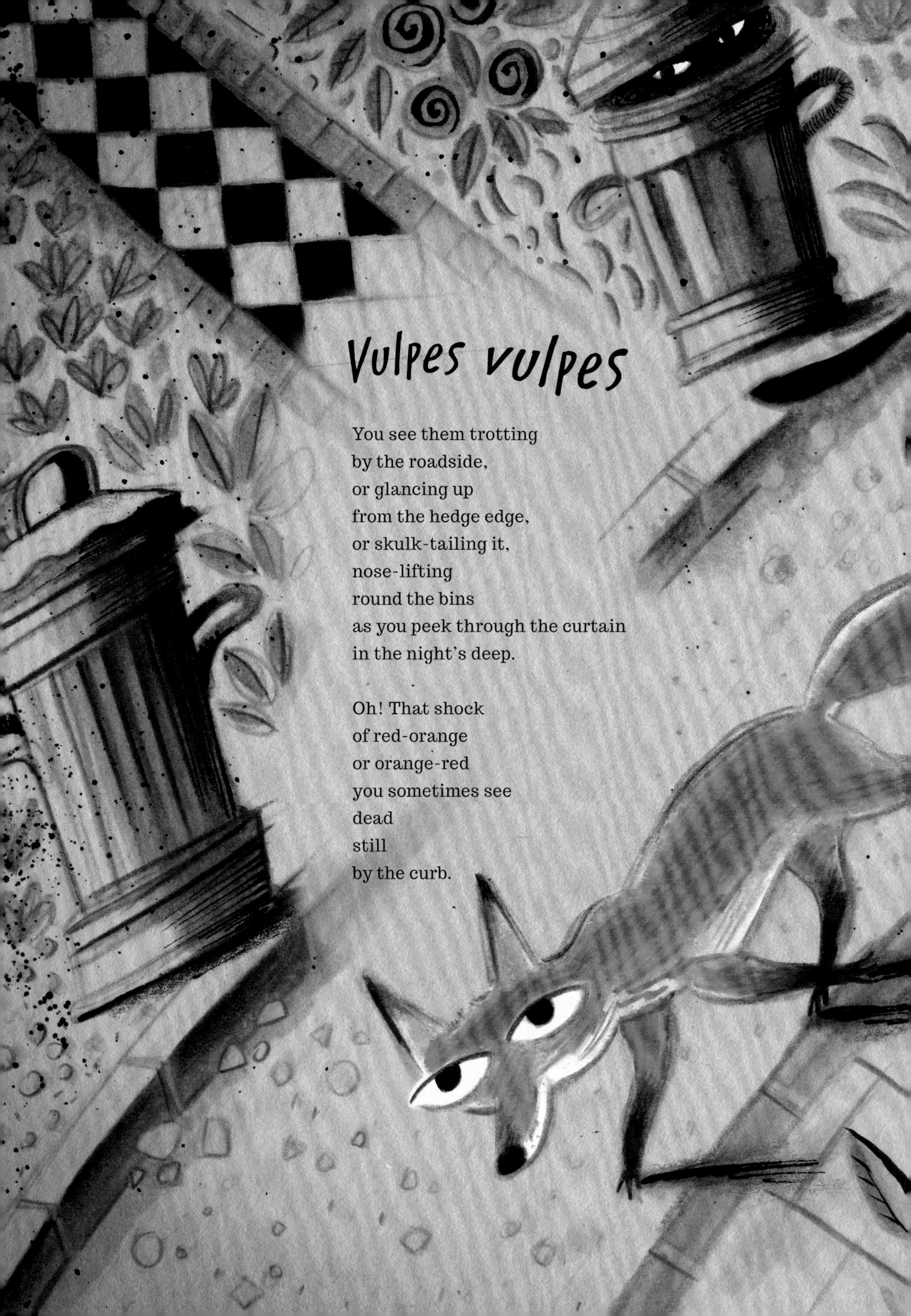

Vulpes vulpes

You see them trotting
by the roadside,
or glancing up
from the hedge edge,
or skulk-tailing it,
nose-lifting
round the bins
as you peek through the curtain
in the night's deep.

Oh! That shock
of red-orange
or orange-red
you sometimes see
dead
still
by the curb.

The Hedgehog

The hedgehog wants a cuddle
in the cold winter night.

He just wants his mummy
to come and hug him tight.

He's woken in the darkness
when the others are asleep.

He's alone and afraid
and the night is slow and deep.

He sniffs and he snuggles
up to his mummy's side.

She wakes with a start and says,
*"Look! If you're going to wriggle and poke
with your prickles every five minutes
you can just go sleep outside, child!
Oh! Stop being so fidgeting annoying!"*

But
this hedgehog
just wants
a cuddle.

The Kilted Koala

If you ask the koala
why it is wearing a kilt
it will chew its eucalyptus leaf
and just stare past you.

Koalas do not like questions.
They like eucalyptus leaves,
hugging trees,
and staring into the distance.

No one knows
why this koala's wearing a kilt,
but sometimes life
is mysterious like that.

How to Avoid a Giant Who Has Escaped from a Nearby Fairy Tale

It's no good looking out the window—
the foot of a giant
gives no warning to those underneath.

There's no use putting up a sign—
unless it's a very high sign
that's big and easy to read.

It's no good trying to run—
the boots of this thing
are as big as small towns.

There's no use trying to hide—
the boot comes squashing,
not searching.

It's no good shouting a warning—
it's a long way up
and your voice is so very small.

In fact there's nothing you can do
to alter the odds.
Nothing, no, nothing at all.

The Ambitious Spider

There's a spider in the bath
and it isn't catching flies.
It's more ambitious than that,
you can see it in all eight eyes.

It spins the stickiest webs
in the gap between the taps,
and all around the overflow,
with the hope that maybe, perhaps

while you are having your bath,
you'll waggle your feet in the air
and get tangled up in the webbing
and get stuck in the spider's snare.

You're unable to escape,
so it'll wander up to your nose
and begin to nibble from there
back down to your entrapped toes.

All they will find in the morning
is a bathtub filled with bones,
and a spider the size of a swan,
emitting satisfied groans.

But it's easy, of course, to be safe,
to avoid the spider's traps:
share a bath with a buddy,
and make them take the end with the taps.

Inside the Anthill

If you've ever wondered, like I have,
what the inside of an anthill looks like
go and lie on the picnic cloth
and pretend to be a cake crumb—

soon an ant and his friends will come,
pick you up and carry you off,
and if you keep very still
you'll soon find yourself inside their hill.

Now I've never done this,
because it's rather a stupid thing to do.
I prefer my clothes to stay clean
and I'm not very good at impressions—

but if it appeals to you
and in your scientific zeal you get carried away,
then please, if you don't mind,
do let me know what you find.

Grow Your Own

Where do you go
to buy lamp post seeds?

I've searched the garden center
fruitlessly for lamp post trees.

Perhaps I'll plant a desk lamp
and water it each night.

In time it'll grow taller.
That's how it works, right?

Holiday

Cuckoos fly south for the winter,
as do many other birds.

They have long holidays—
a whole season.

I wonder, do they stay in hotels
or in rented cottages, or camp out?

Do they lie by the pool
or go exploring,

or take day trips to museums,
and do they eat as much as they can

from the buffet breakfast
to avoid having to buy lunch,

like we did
when we went on holiday as kids?

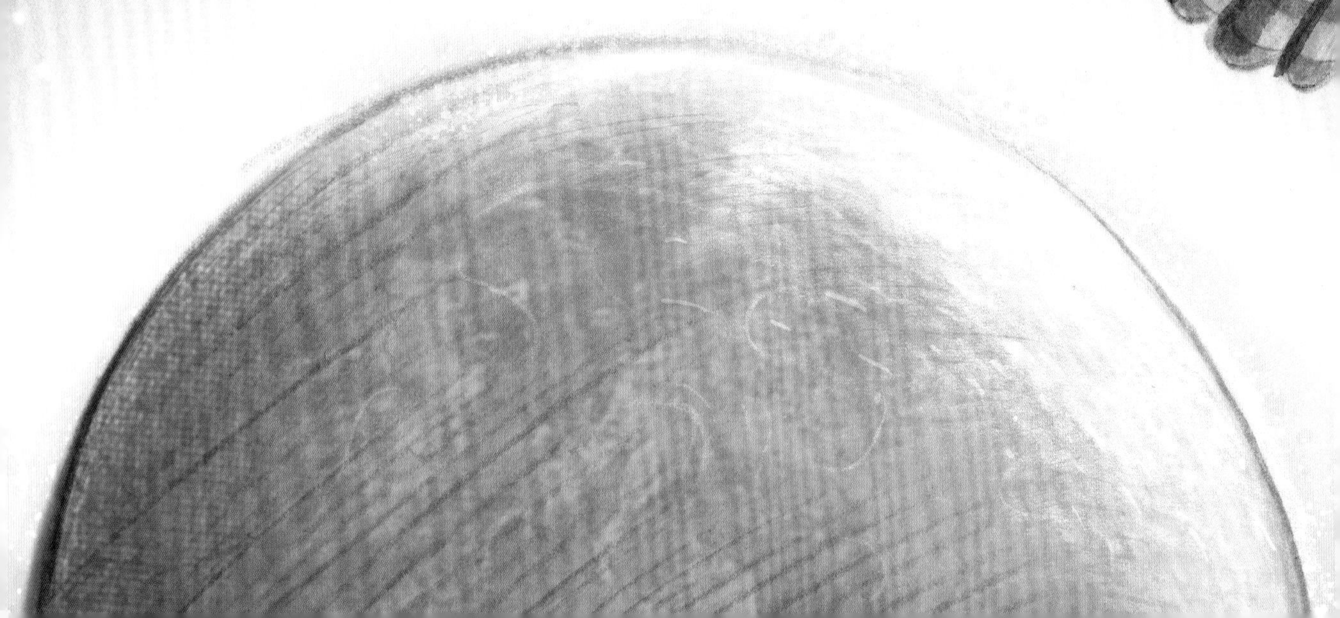

Earth Song

Some of it is brown
and some of it is green.
Some of it is blue
and some is in between.

Some of it is local,
depending where you are.
Some of it is reachable
in a motorcar.

Some of it is dusty
and some of it is swampy.
Some of it is flattish
and some of it is lumpy.

Some of it's in darkness
and some of it's alight.
Some of it is frozen hard
and shining blinding white.

Some of it is poisoned
and some of it is dying.
Some of it is silent
and some of it is crying.

Some of it is going
and some of it is gone.
Some of it . . .

More Further Notes for the Reader

Sometimes it can be hard to know what to say when people ask you for your advice.

Well, dear reader, there is no need for a blank brain or an unadvised friend ever again!

All you need is a six-sided die and the chart opposite.

Simply roll your dice for each of the columns (Beginning, Middle, and End) and read the corresponding bits-of-a-sentence in order (Beginning, Middle, and End) and you will create a brand new, almost unique piece of advice. (This machine makes 216 different pieces of advice, but if you swap in some of the bonus entries from the box below it'll make even more.)

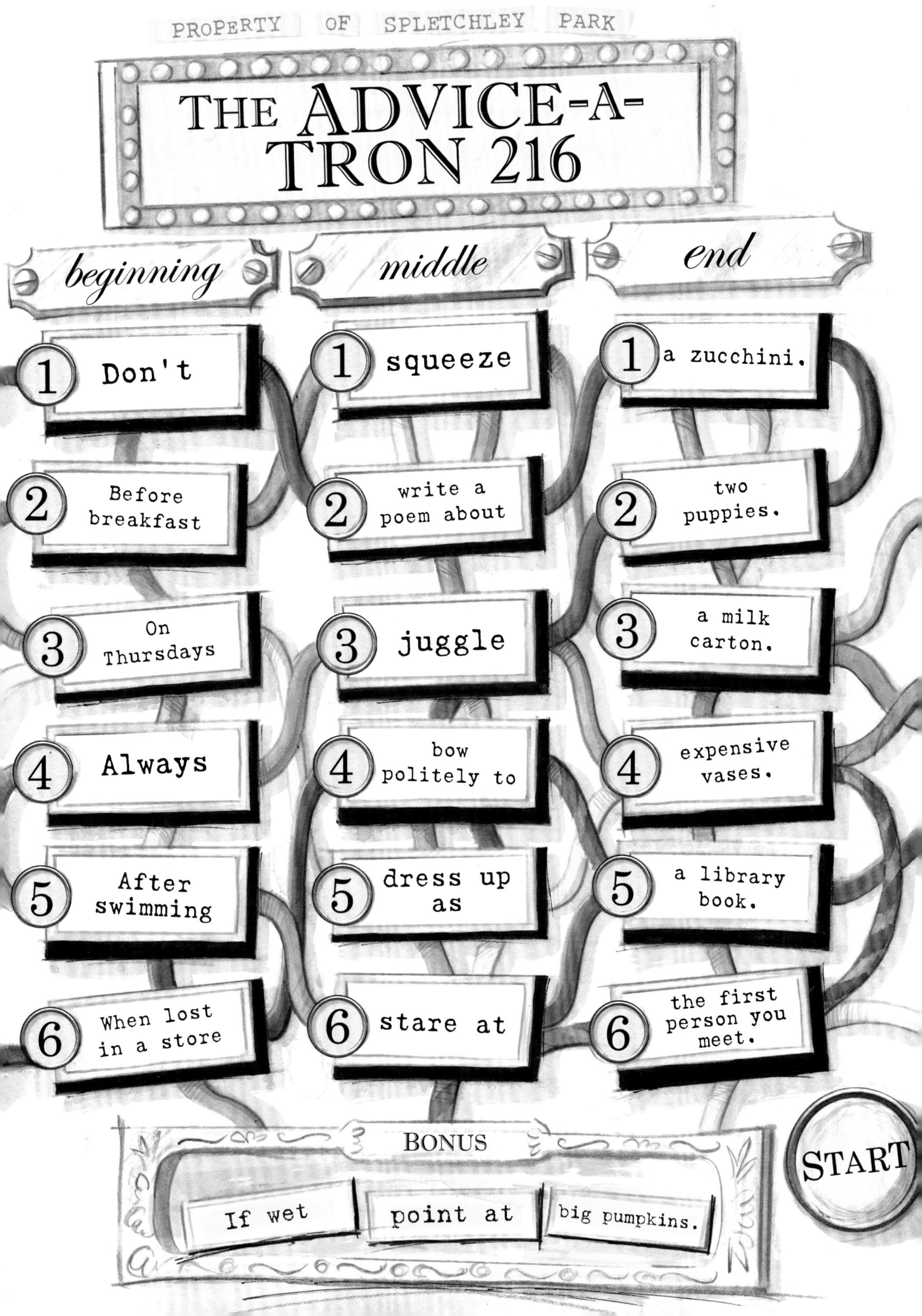
PROPERTY OF SPLETCHLEY PARK
THE ADVICE-A-TRON 216
beginning
middle
end
1 Don't
2 Before breakfast
3 On Thursdays
4 Always
5 After swimming
6 When lost in a store
1 squeeze
2 write a poem about
3 juggle
4 bow politely to
5 dress up as
6 stare at
1 a zucchini.
2 two puppies.
3 a milk carton.
4 expensive vases.
5 a library book.
6 the first person you meet.
BONUS
If wet
point at
big pumpkins.
START

SECTION 3

Advice mainly relating to school life, onions, and general-knowledge-type stuff

The Value of an Onion

Always keep an onion handy.
They're great for self-defense.

If someone tries to beat you up,
whip out your onion and say:

"Look! Behold! An onion!
The Great Onion of Dreams!

The Magic Onion of Derek!*
Stare upon it and shudder!

For it is an astonishing onion!
An onion of Power and Fear!

Gaze upon its majesty in awe!
Tremble before this onion!"

And then, when the bully's thoroughly confused,
kick them in the shin and run away.

*Insert your own name, or another name of your choice that you think sounds impressive.

Illustrator's note:
Here are some names
I found earlier.

Norman
Theresa
Katy
Priya
Chris

The
MAGIC ONION
OF DEREK
KING OF VEG
Look on my layers, ye mortals, and despair.

The Problem of the Wrong Oblong

My oblong's gone wrong.
(Look, just over there.)
Two sides are too short . . .

I'll call it a square.

Problem solved.

The Day I Ate My Pencil

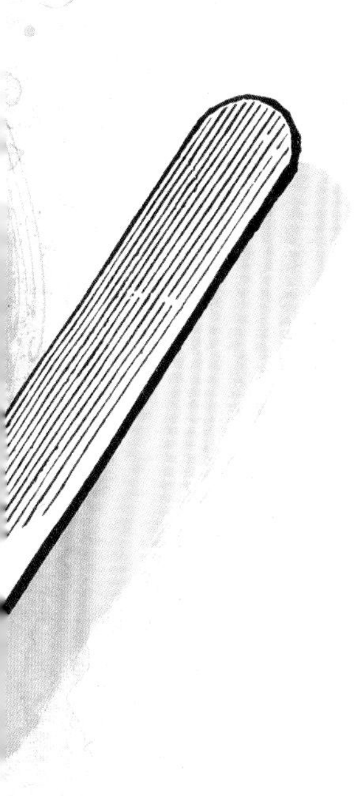

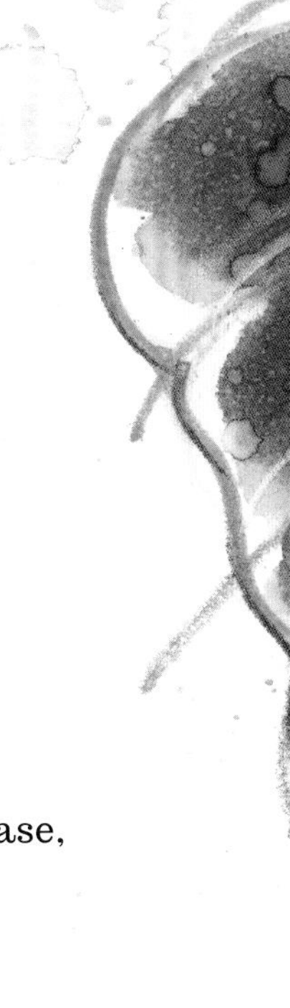

My pencil was blunt
at the front.

It refused to make a
mark on the paper.

My teacher came round
and frowned.

“Why are you poking your page
with a sausage roll?” she said.

I must say
I learned a lesson that day:

Never muddle your lunch box and pencil case,
because wood and graphite don’t taste

very nice.
(I only ever did this twice.)

Inside

It might look to you
like I'm sat on the sofa,
but look closer: *I'm not there.*

It might look to you
like I'm lying on my bed,
but look closer: *I'm not there.*

It might look to you
like I'm strapped in the back seat,
but look closer: *I'm not there.*

Where am I?
I'm inside.
I'm between the covers.
I'm in so deep.
I'm through the paper door.
I'm breathing the air of other worlds.
I'm exploring.
I'm reading

and I can't hear you anymore.

Dear Diary

Dear diary.
Today I wrote in you.
Dear dairy.
Today I had a pint of milk.

Drear diary.
Today was rubbish and boring.
Drear dairy.
Today the cows were gloomy.

Deer diary.
Today I ran away from a hunter.
Deer dairy.
Today I milked an antelope.

Idea daily.
Today I thought of something interesting.
Ideal diary.
This stuff writes itself.

Dear diarrhea-y.
Expensive carpet ruined.

Belt Advice

Snakes
don't make
great belts.

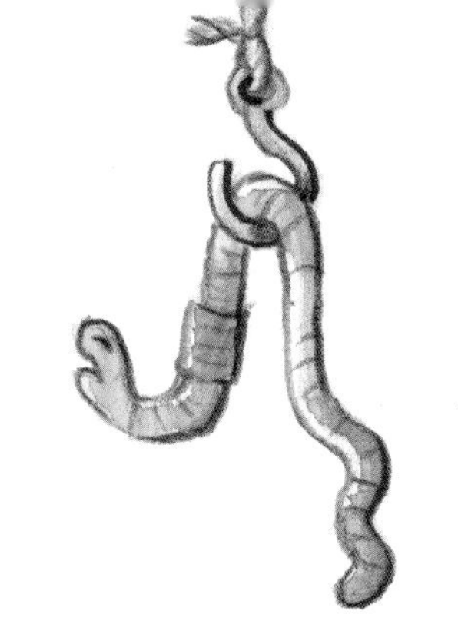

You know what else?

Worms don't either.

Don't be tempted
to sift mud
and string one
through the loops
on your trousers.

That way disaster lies.

One extra spoonful of pudding
and your worm will pop,
split,
and your trousers will flop
to the floor
as your belt
crawls off in two
different
directions.

The same goes for spaghetti,
except for the "crawling off in two different directions"
bit.

Spaghetti doesn't crawl,
which is why it's ideal
for sandwiches.

In case I was unclear
at the start:
Snakes?
Don't.

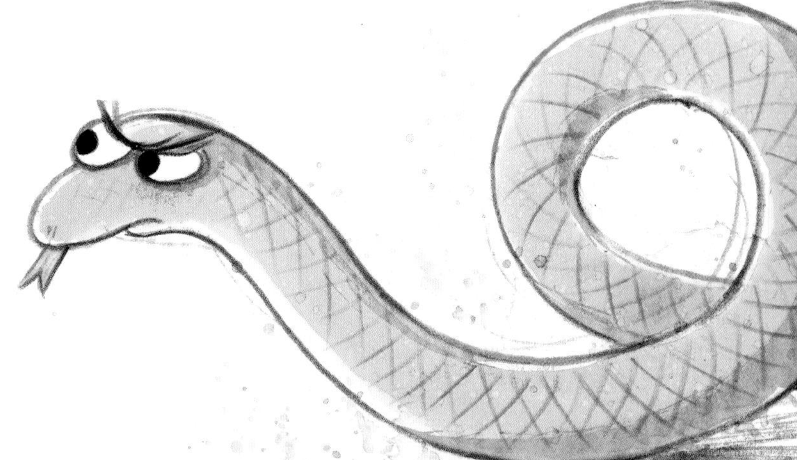

Eagles and Elephants

An eagle is not an elephant,
but they do both lay eggs
(except the elephant).

An elephant is not an envelope,
but they do both like mud
(except the envelope).

An envelope is not an engagement ring,
but they do both live in pillar boxes
(except the engagement ring).

An engagement ring is not an earlobe,
but they do both like to hug a finger
(except the earlobe).

An earlobe is not an evening at the theater,
but they do both dangle
(except the evening at the theater).

An evening at the theater is not an eagle,
but I imagine you already knew that.

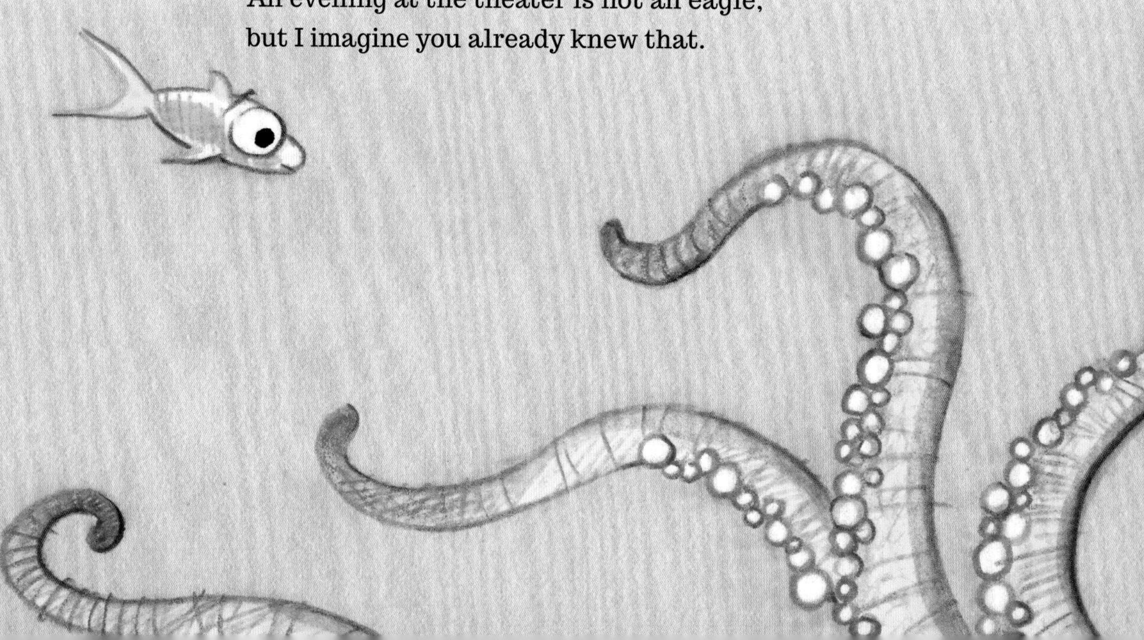

Testing Hats

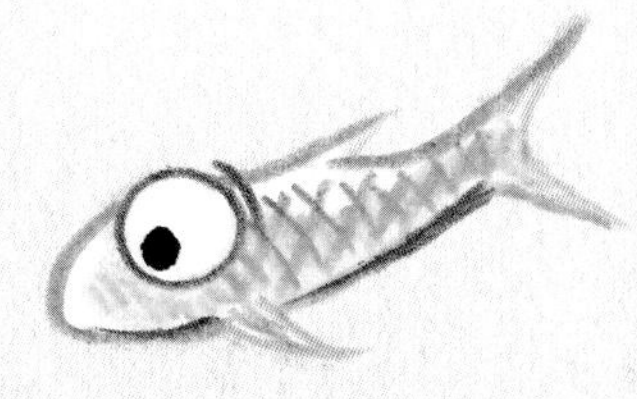

I put a bird's nest on my head.
It's now a bird's-nest hat.
I have to stay upright
so that the eggs don't fall out.

I put an angry cat on my head.
It's now an angry-cat hat.
I have to stay very still
because the cat is very angry.

I put an octopus on my head.
It's now an octopus hat.
I have to hold my breath
since octopuses live underwater.

I put a librarian on my head.
It's now a librarian hat.
She points out that this
is a very silly way to test hats.

So, I put some air on my head
above the hair on my head.
It's an airy-hairy hat
and it fits just fine.

Zombie Monitor

I was the Zombie Monitor
at our school.

I walked behind Mr. Sockett,
the zombie PE teacher,
and when a bit fell off him
I put it in my basket,
and Mr. Hunchday,
the Home Economics teacher,
would sew it back on at lunchtime.

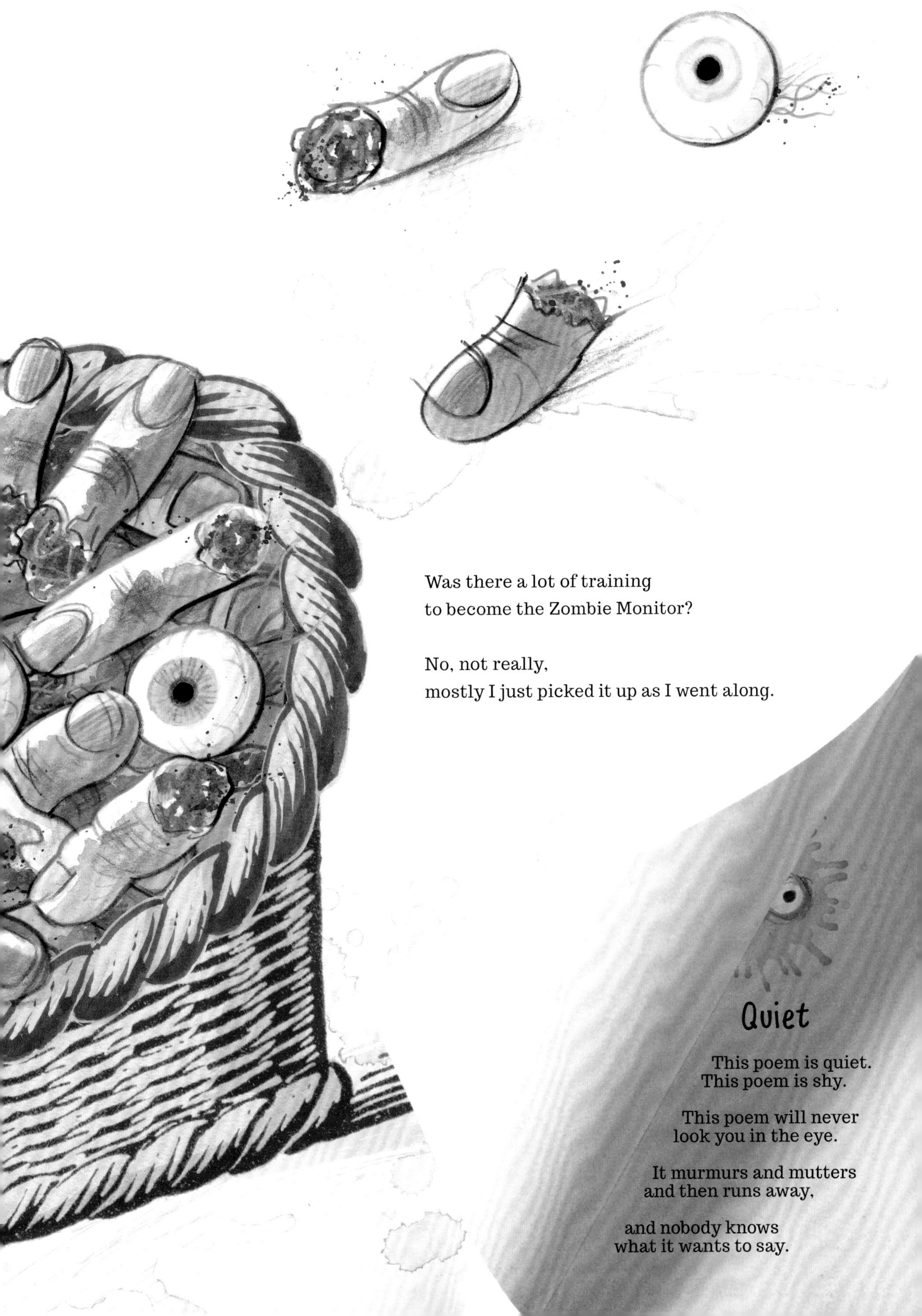

Was there a lot of training
to become the Zombie Monitor?

No, not really,
mostly I just picked it up as I went along.

Quiet

This poem is quiet.
This poem is shy.

This poem will never
look you in the eye.

It murmurs and mutters
and then runs away,

and nobody knows
what it wants to say.

Moon

Coming out of school
and there she is—
a chalk-smudge
finger dab
of white on blue.

You can see the sky through it
like
your mother's heart
through her frown.

Alonely

The pea in the pod
when the peapod's been podded,
but not podded perfectly well.

The pee in the pool
when the pool has been peed in—
a brief cloud of yellow, no smell.

Unloved and unheard from,
forgotten at best,
ignored in the playground, or worse—

remembered and noticed,
a target embodied,
surrounded, then prodded, then burst.

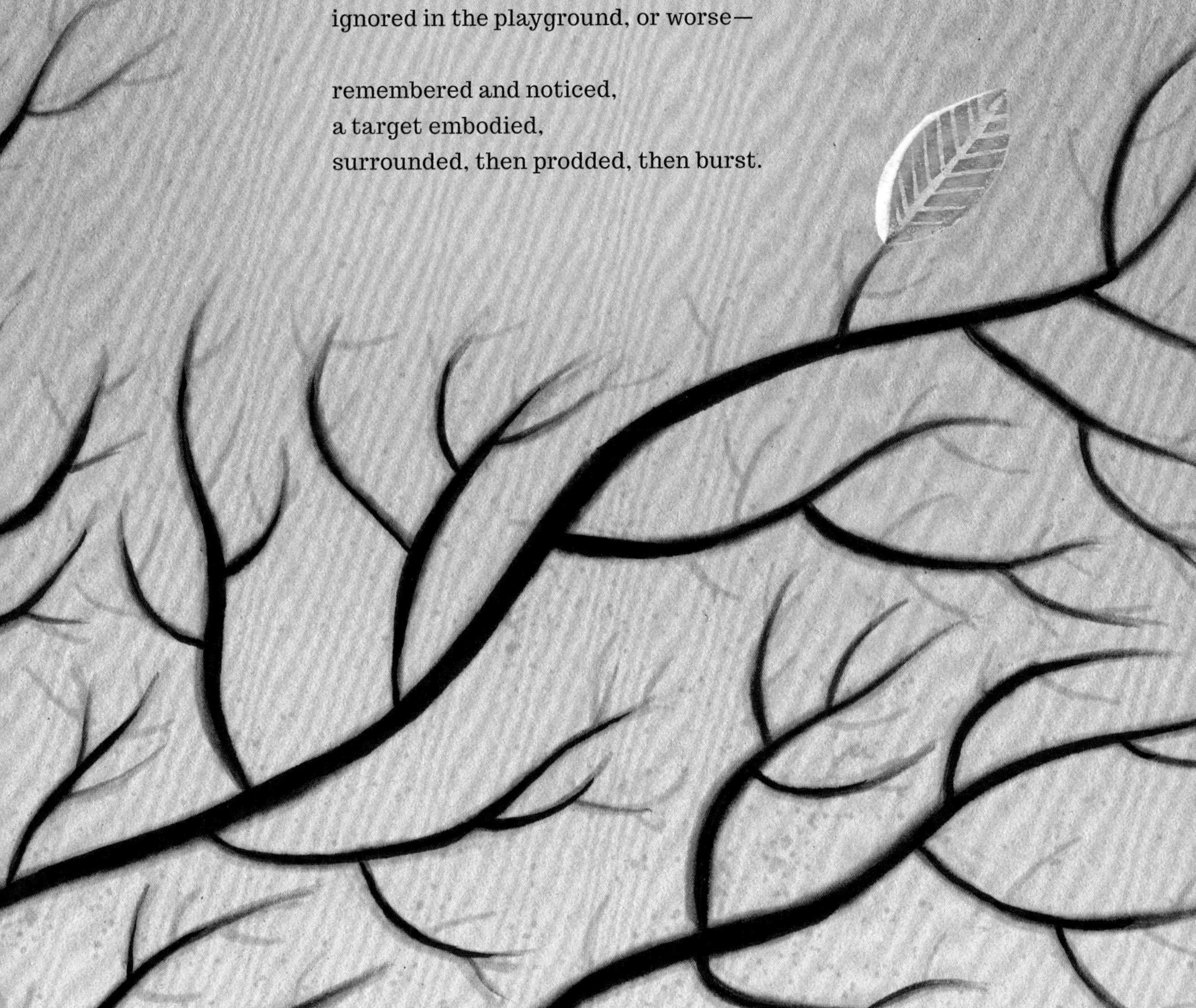

WEEK
WEDNESDAY
TUESDAY
MONDAY

Wednesday's the High Point of the Week

If the week is geography
then Wednesday
must be the hill in the middle.

You've spent days
climbing up,
hauling yourself forward,

and now you stand surveying
the world around you,
everything sparkling.

And from here it's all downhill,
freewheeling
toward the weekend.

(Which isn't to say,
in case a teacher reads this poem,
that Thursday and Friday

should be careless, carefree
work-shy days.
But they are, almost, the weekend, so . . .)

C3

All at Sea

I've nacht
gacht
a lacht
to say
about the yacht,
except:
"Whacht's
going on with the spelling?"

Even More Further Notes for the Reader

We were thinking about where we get advice from, especially when we're very young, and it's often from fairy tales and fables.

Take the ever-popular story of the Three Big Pigs, for example:

Once upon a time there were three big pigs. Actually, that's whatever the opposite of an exaggeration is . . . they weren't just big, *they were* huge, *maybe even bigger than that.*

One day a wolf came along and she was a hungry wolf. Oh, she hadn't eaten for weeks, and her tummy was rumbling and she took one look at these enormous *pigs and thought to herself, "Yummy."*

So she put on a hat, which she thought made her look not quite so wolfish, and walked up to the first pig, lying on his bed of straw, and she said, "Oh, great big piggy, can I nibble your leg? I'm so famished and you do have four of them, all juicy, luscious and plump."

But the first pig was fast asleep and didn't hear what the wolf-disguised-as-a-wolf-wearing-a-hat had said, and he just rolled over in the middle of a dream about wallowing in beautiful mud.

The wolf-disguised-as-a-wolf-wearing-a-hat was squashed dead flat and that was the end of that.

And so the three big pigs lived happily ever after, until the day the farmer came with his . . . but that's another story for another day, my dear little one.

In that old story we learn three things:

- Firstly, a hat isn't a good disguise.
- Secondly, let sleeping pigs lie.
- And thirdly, never say how many things you're putting on a list until you've actually thought of the things you're going to put on the list, otherwise you'll be stuck with a weird one at the end.

Unfortunately, since this is a book of poems and drawings, we don't have the time or the space to go over all our favorite fables or fairy tales, but take a moment or two to think of one of your favorites before turning the page.

SECTION 4

Advice mainly relating to the human condition, dreams, and miscellaneous other subjects that didn't fit elsewhere

For A.F.
a little something
from Mini

Expectations

I expected a surprise
for my birthday.

Imagine my surprise
when I didn't get one.

Slippery Hitch

Double Cross

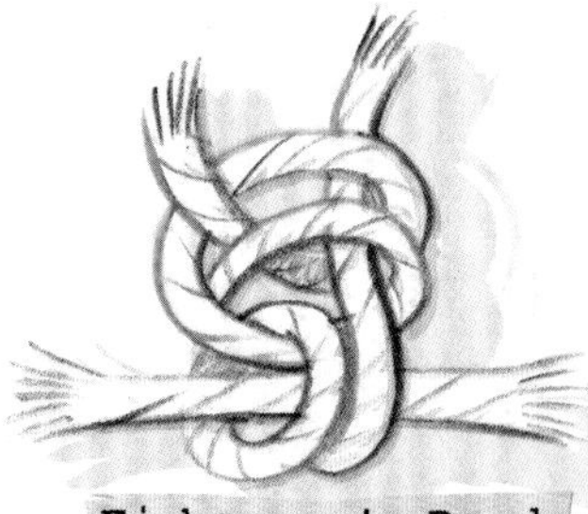
Fisherman's Bend

Flippery Twitch

Cross your heart and hope to fly,
poke a postman in the eye.

Cross your liver all day long,
cats and dogs will sing a song.

Cross your lungs with strawberry jam,
push a pickle in a pram.

Cross your road and shut your eyes,
this is not a sensible idea.

Fisherman's Twist

Fisherman's Eye

Granny Knot

Fisherman's Nostril

Double Overhand

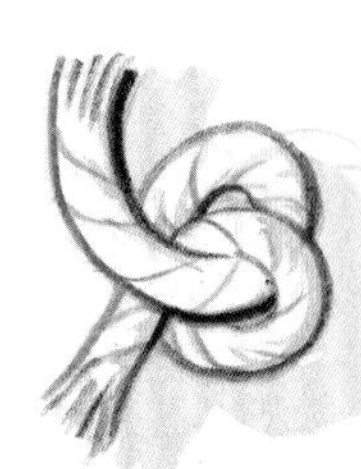
Afraid Knot

Sheepshank

Double Underhand

Why Knot

Lambshank

Utterly Underhand

Ikidyou Knot

Knot Knots

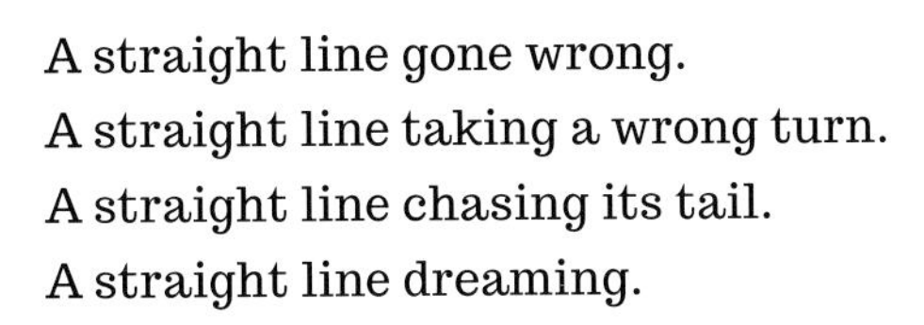

A straight line gone wrong.
A straight line taking a wrong turn.
A straight line chasing its tail.
A straight line dreaming.

A string looking inside itself.
A string listening to its own story.
A string with no one else to hug.
A string dancing.

Follow the thread under the hill.
Follow the thread round the houses.
Follow the thread down the rabbit hole.
Then untie it and start again.

Fruit Flip

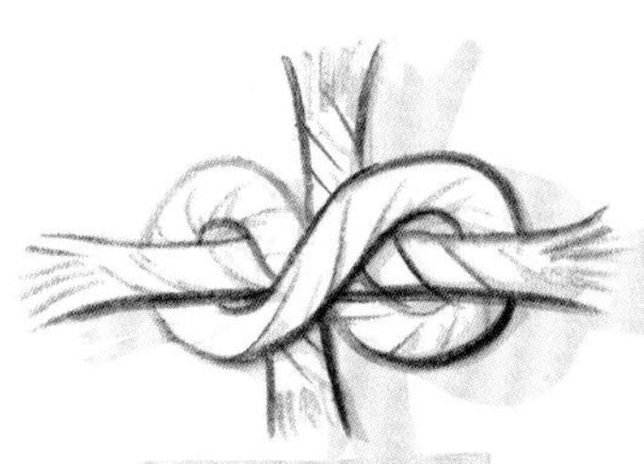

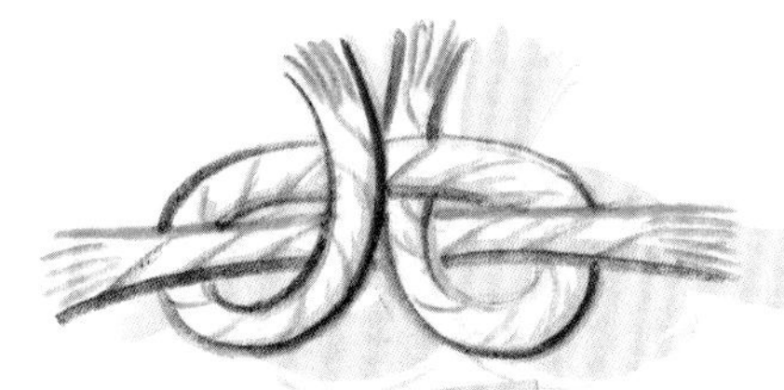

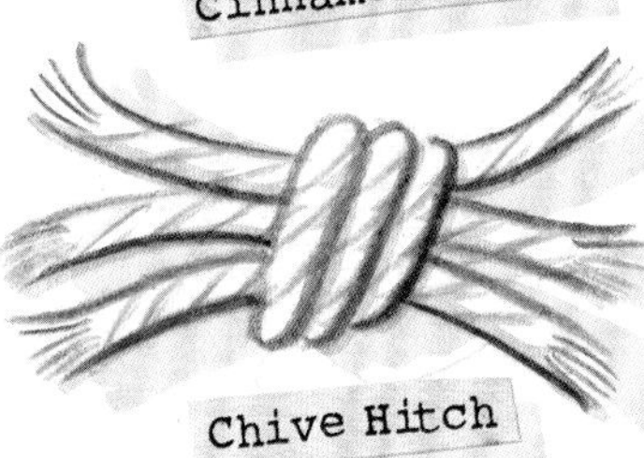

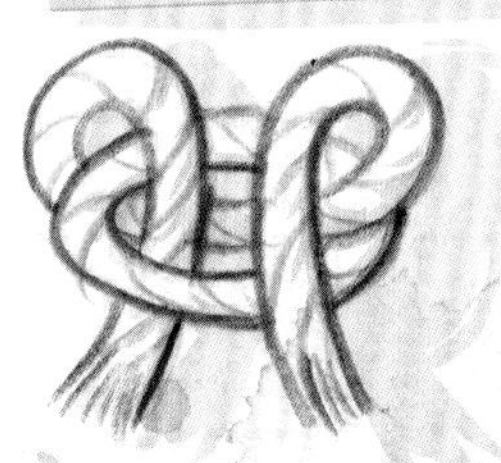

THE WORLD*

* collected by Mini Grey

In the Dark

Lying in bed
a little afraid
listening to the noises
  in the dark
    in the night
  in the house
the squeaks, ticks, and bumps
I remember what mum said:

think of the house as a ship
  in the night
    on the sea
    with the rigging
  creaking above
as it rocks on the waves

it's so peaceful out at sea
  no ghosts
    no monsters
    no burglars
  nothing scary
all noises explained away simply

and I lie in bed
no longer afraid
just, ever so slightly, seasick instead

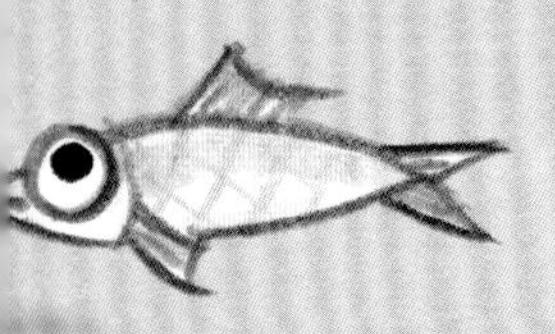

Clouds

Clouds are loud when thunder rolls,
when lightning snaps
and the rainstorm pours down,

but mostly, mostly they say nothing,
piled up or stretched thin,
long fingers pointing always away.

Silently they drift above our heads,
bulky huge light oceans,
filled with invisible impossible fish of imagination.

An empty blue sky is a lonely sky,
too big, too wide.
A black bird-speck circles, too high.

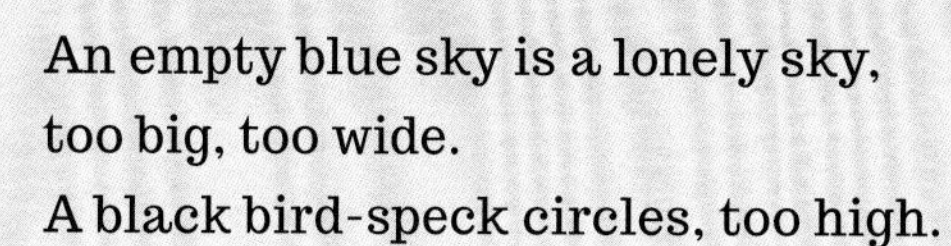

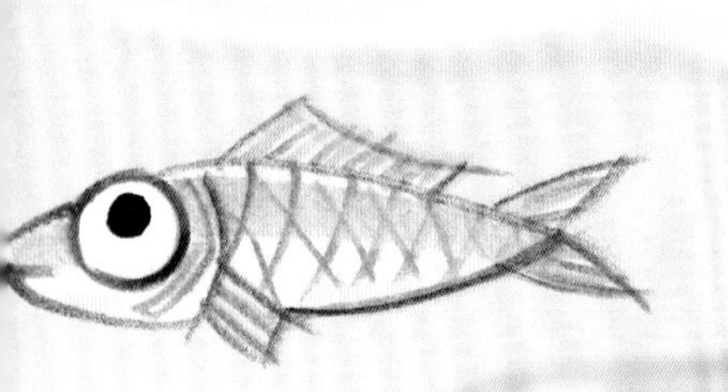

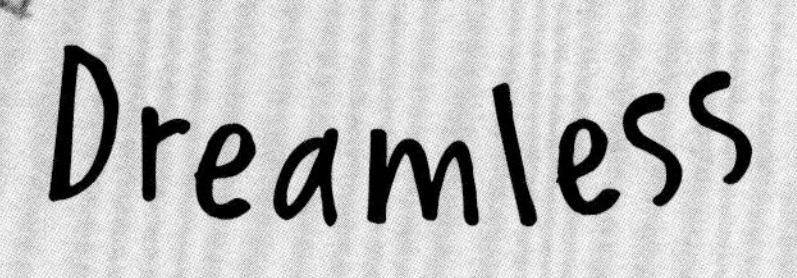

Dreamless

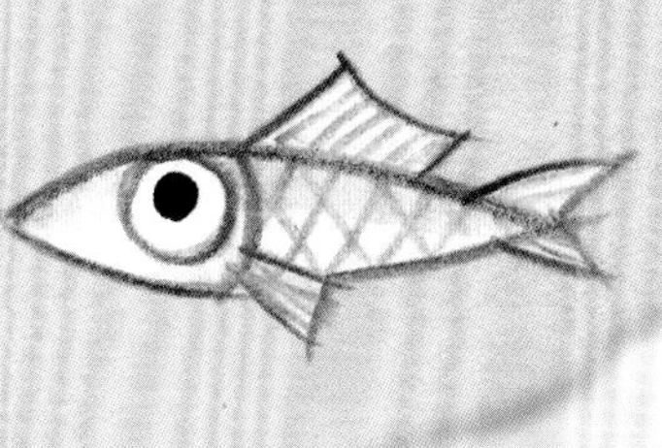

It's a long night
that has no dreams in it.

It's a long dark night
without the movie show
rolling round your head.

It's a long dark dull night
without unexpected
unexplained
unlikely adventures

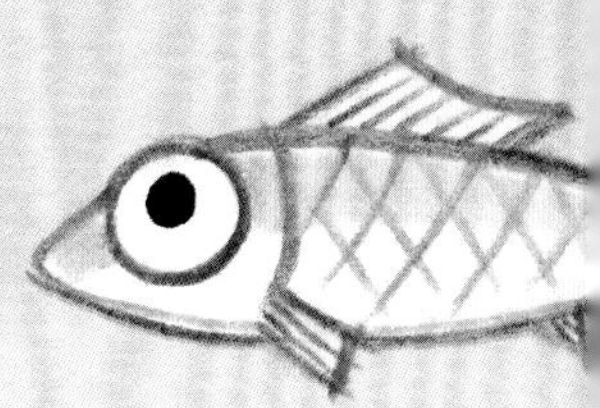

such as flying over the town
startling starlings
and perplexing pigeons,

or eating all the cakes
the baker bakes
and scoffing all the sweets
and chocolate treats
that litter the dreamer's streets.

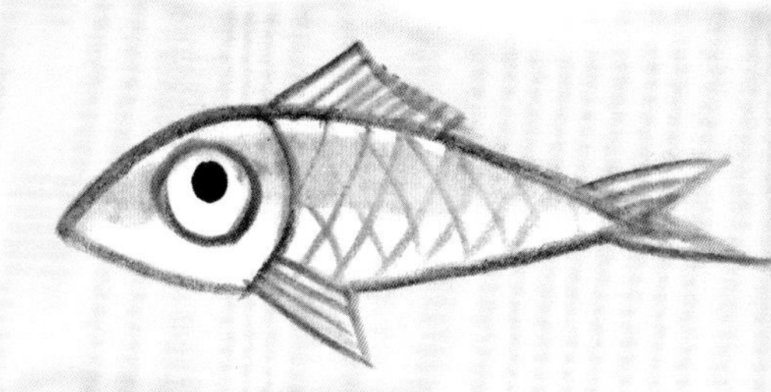

It's a dull night
with no dreams in.

Just darkness from dusk
to morning's first light,
and the sound of snoring
and the smell of duvet.

It's a dull day
with no dreams in either.

The Idea of It

They ask:
Where do you find your ideas?

I say:
There's a shop
down an alley
in a town,
that's only open
once a year
on a Thursday
when the moon is full
and a cat hums Mozart on TV,
where ideas are sold
to poets
and writers
on a first come
first inspired basis
for reasonable sums of money.

And they say:
Really?

And I say:
No. Not really.
But it's an idea.

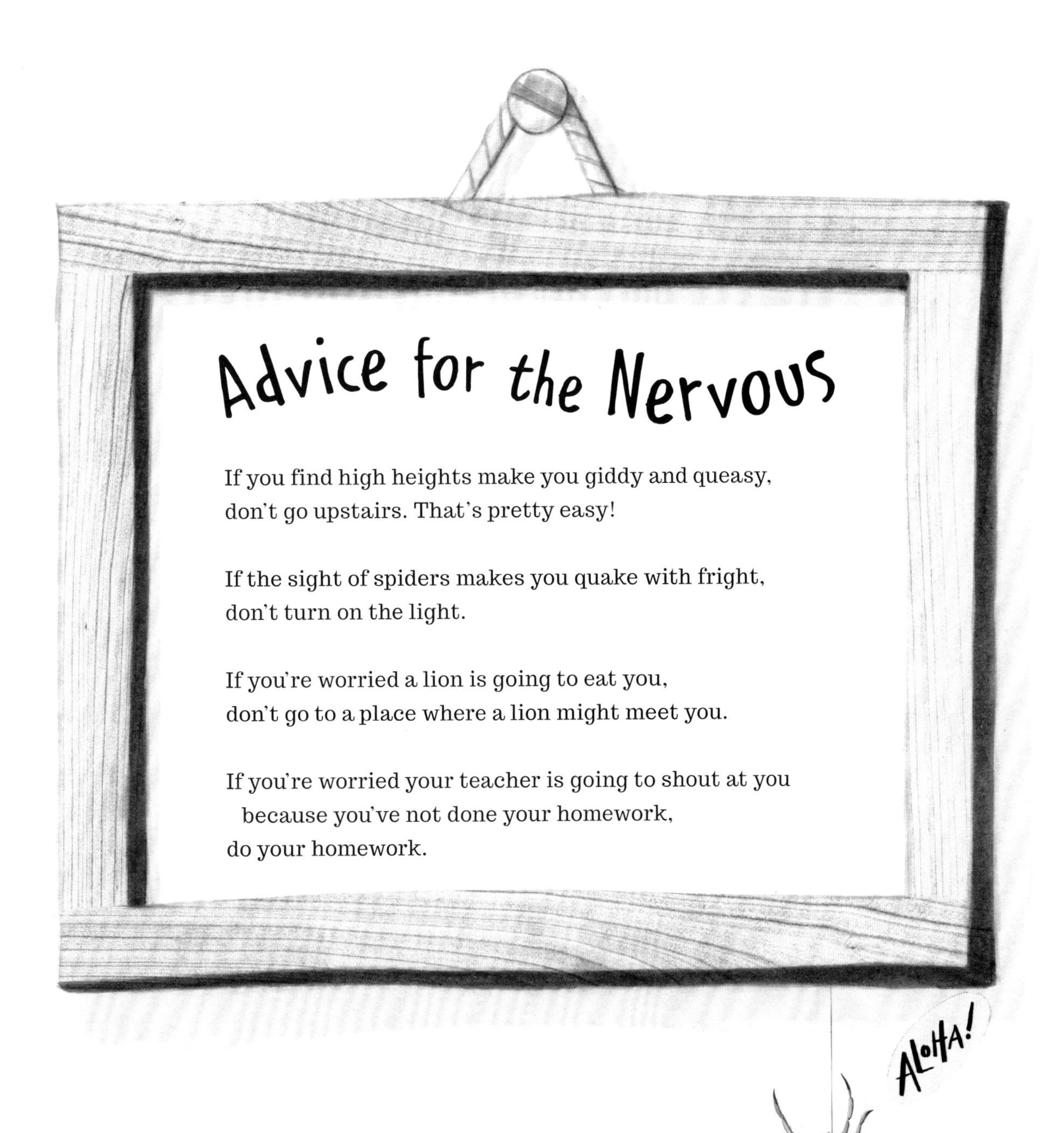

Advice for the Nervous

If you find high heights make you giddy and queasy,
don't go upstairs. That's pretty easy!

If the sight of spiders makes you quake with fright,
don't turn on the light.

If you're worried a lion is going to eat you,
don't go to a place where a lion might meet you.

If you're worried your teacher is going to shout at you
  because you've not done your homework,
do your homework.

Bin

If you're going to rummage
in bins

choose the bin you rummage in
wisely.

Don't rummage in any old bin
or a bin

you find by the side of the road.
Those bins

will be full of horrible things,
smelly things,

broken things that people threw away.
Instead

rummage in the bins belonging to
rich people:

the sort who chuck out their fivers
when they're torn,

or their tenners when they're crumpled.
These are the bins

for diving in, or so my dad taught me.
And so far

they haven't caught me.

Silences

Cat paws through the garden.
Butterflies in flight.
Morning daisies yawning.
The slowly falling night.

Snow before it's trodden.
Books before they're read.
The moon when freshly risen.
A secret left unsaid.

Clouds not ready to rain yet.
Fresh-stretching apple pips.
That moment between tick and tock.
Your finger-hushed lips.

Sing a Happy Song

We like to sing opera,
my sister and me—
I am the fat lady
and she's the man who wears a hat
to confuse everyone
into thinking he's someone else, because hats do that.

We like to sing opera,
wherever we are—
our favorite places to sing are:
one, at the dentist's;
two, in the car when it's stopped in a traffic jam;
three, in assembly;
four, in the bath;
and, five, when we're bored.

We like to sing opera
loudly, passionately, dramatically—
but Mum said not to mention any of that
when she left us on your doorstep
and drove away,
Mr. Orphanage-Owner.

So do you mind if we stay?
Only . . . I feel a song coming on . . .

Poet at the Disco

I've got a special suit,
it's entirely made of ants,
it tickles when I wear it:
now, watch me dance . . .

Numb and Number

My sister punched my arm
 until it went numb.
Then she punched my leg
 until it went number.
Then she punched my other arm
 until it went numbest.
Then she punched my other leg
 until I fell over.

My sister's a jerk,
 but I'll get her back one day.

When she's not looking
 I'll grow up
and become a super-successful poet
 and I'll write a scathing poem
about what a jerk she was
 when we were kids.

And then I'll hide,
 just in case she reads it
and decides to punch
 my writing arm
  until it falls off.

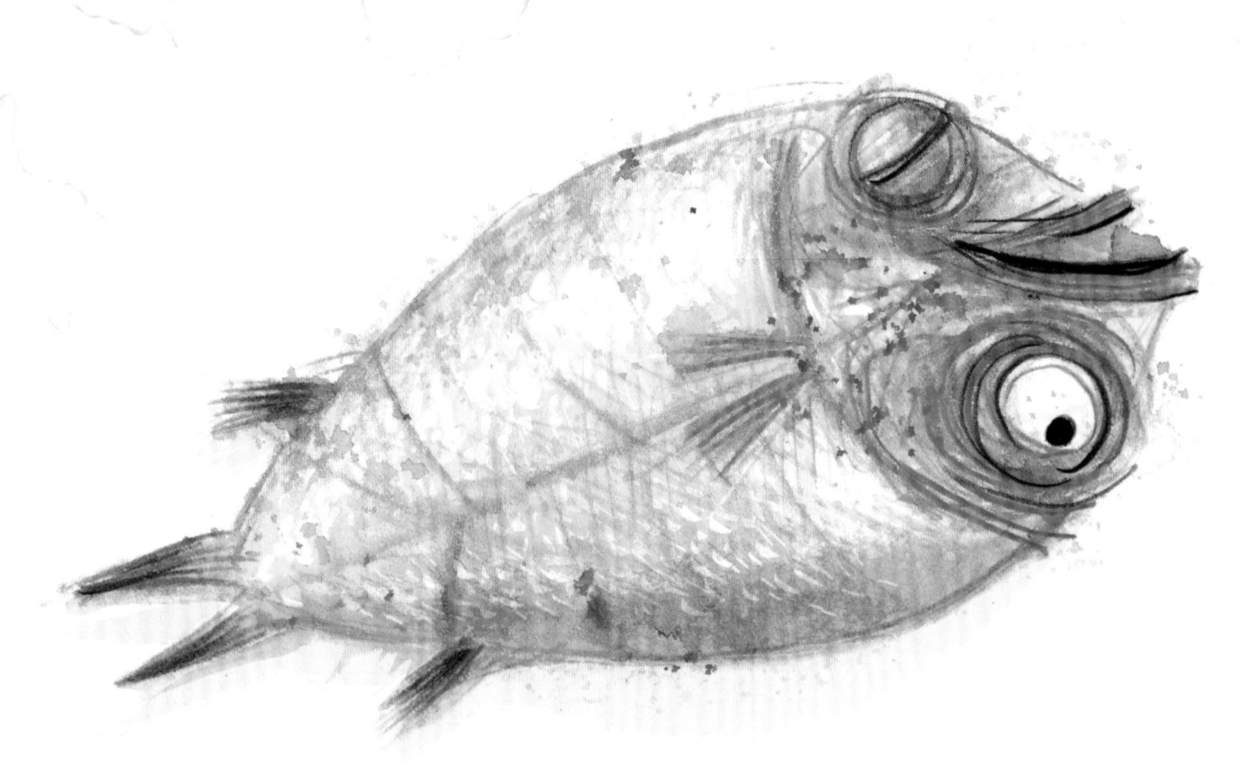

Useless

I feel as useful as a kipper that's been kept in a kettle,
as useful as a conker in your socks,
as useful as a top hat that's been stuffed with orange jelly
and then balanced on the head of a fox.

I feel as useful as an ostrich on the number eighteen bus,
as useful as a desert in a pool,
as useful as a sausage that you've asked for assistance
with the homework that you've brought home from school.

I feel as useful as a cabbage that's learned to play cricket,
as useful as a llama on the moon,
as useful as a trifle that is sitting on the sideboard
saying "Eat me" out of sight of a spoon.

But enough about me,
let's talk about you . . .

The Poet Gives Some Free Advice

Squeeze some grapes
and you'll get grape juice.
Open the gate
and you'll let some sheep loose.

Set an alarm
and you'll wake up on time.
Cuddle a hedgehog
and you won't feel fine.

Eat only butter
and you'll probably get fat.
Sit on someone's head
and you'll look like a hat.

Butler

If I had a butler
I'd be forever
climbing out the window
sneaking round
to the front of the house
and ringing
the bell
in order to have him
open the door
and say,
"Yes, sir?
How may I help you?"
in that slow,
unflappable voice
that sounds so much
like yawning.

The Exaggerator

I used to aggerate
all the time.
Oh, constantly,
endlessly,
aggerating about this, that or the other,
left, right, and center.

I was the best aggerator
you'd have ever met,
had you met me back then.

I was tremendous,
with a capital Tree.

But it was very tiring.
And after a while it got a bit boring.

So now I've given it up.
Don't aggerate anymore.
Haven't aggerated for about a million years.
No, actually, it's probably more like a billion . . .
And a half . . .

Two Quick Tips

Never go shoplifting.
They're heavy things
and one accidental slip
might lead to a drop of the shop
and could chop
off a fingertip or two.

On the other hand,
never go shiplofting either.
Hoisting a boat in the air
will drop seaweed in your hair,
fish on your head
and if your scarf gets caught
in the propellers, kid, you're dead.

Say Something Nice

Every now and then
say something nice.

Say it to a friend.

Say it to a teacher.

Say it to your sister
or brother,
your father or mother.

Say something nice like:

You remind me of flowers.

Or:

Your hair is like fresh bread.

Or:

I like sausages.

Or:

You're better than asparagus.

Or:

I like you more than Simon.

Just something nice
to make them feel good.

The world is sometimes gray
and things go wrong,
but a kind word
and a smile
can turn it back around.

Say something nice like:

That wasn't a very good poem,
but I liked it when it stopped.

Bath Poem

If there's a fire in the house
don't scream and run and shout.
Just sit tight in the bath
and splash it all about.

Umbrella Poem

Look at the fella
with the umbrella.

To him the rain
isn't a pain.

The light shower
lacks the power

to get
his hair wet.

It feels good,
this bundle of wire and cloth and wood.

But it won't help
when he falls in the river.

Jumper

A jumper's an awkward thing.

When it's cold
you try to get yourself inside it.
But first
you have to catch it.

From floor to bed it jumps.
From bed to wardrobe it jumps.
From wardrobe to floor it jumps.
Out the door it jumps.
Across the landing it jumps.

With you
racing,
bounding,
leaping after it.

Eventually you grab it,
catch one of its flapping sleeves
in your fingers
and wrestle it to the ground.
Pin it down.

And do you know what?
All that exercise has made you hot.
Far too hot to wear a jumper.
You'd now much better suit a sweater.

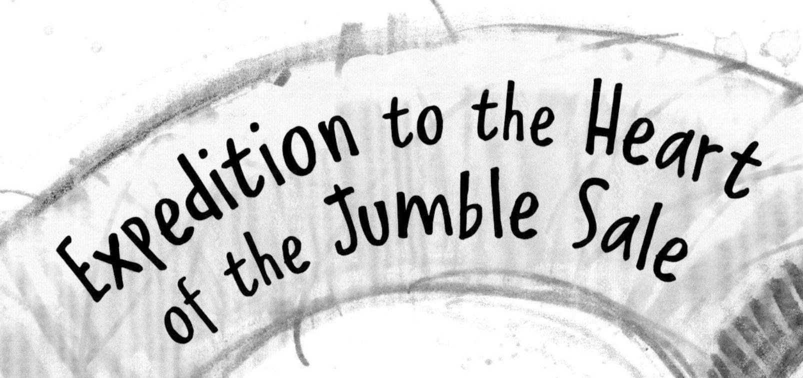

Expedition to the Heart of the Jumble Sale

I'd like to buy a parrot, please.
And an anteater.
And some vines, if you don't mind.
And two monkeys.
And some bananas, and guavas.
And can I get some termites
to go with the anteater?
And the noise of birds up in the canopy,
shouting and singing, please.
And snakes. Lots of tasty snakes.
And do you have any clearings
with the ruins of ancient lost cities in?
I'd quite like one of those too, please.

I think you're a bit confused.
This is a jumble sale, not a jungle sale.

Oh.
Oops.
My mistake. Sorry.
I'll just have one small jumble
then.
To take away.

That'll be 50 pence.

Thank you.

The Point

Point to the sky.
Draw a line from your finger.
It'll go on forever.
Through light and through darkness.
Past astronauts sleeping.
Past clouds and past planets.
Through silence unmeasured.
Through time uncounted.
A line that's so long.
It will never stop going.
Long after you've dropped
your hand to your side.
And gone back indoors.
That line is still sketching.
Onward and outward.
Universe threading.
Oh, your finger's a marvel.
Take care where you point it.

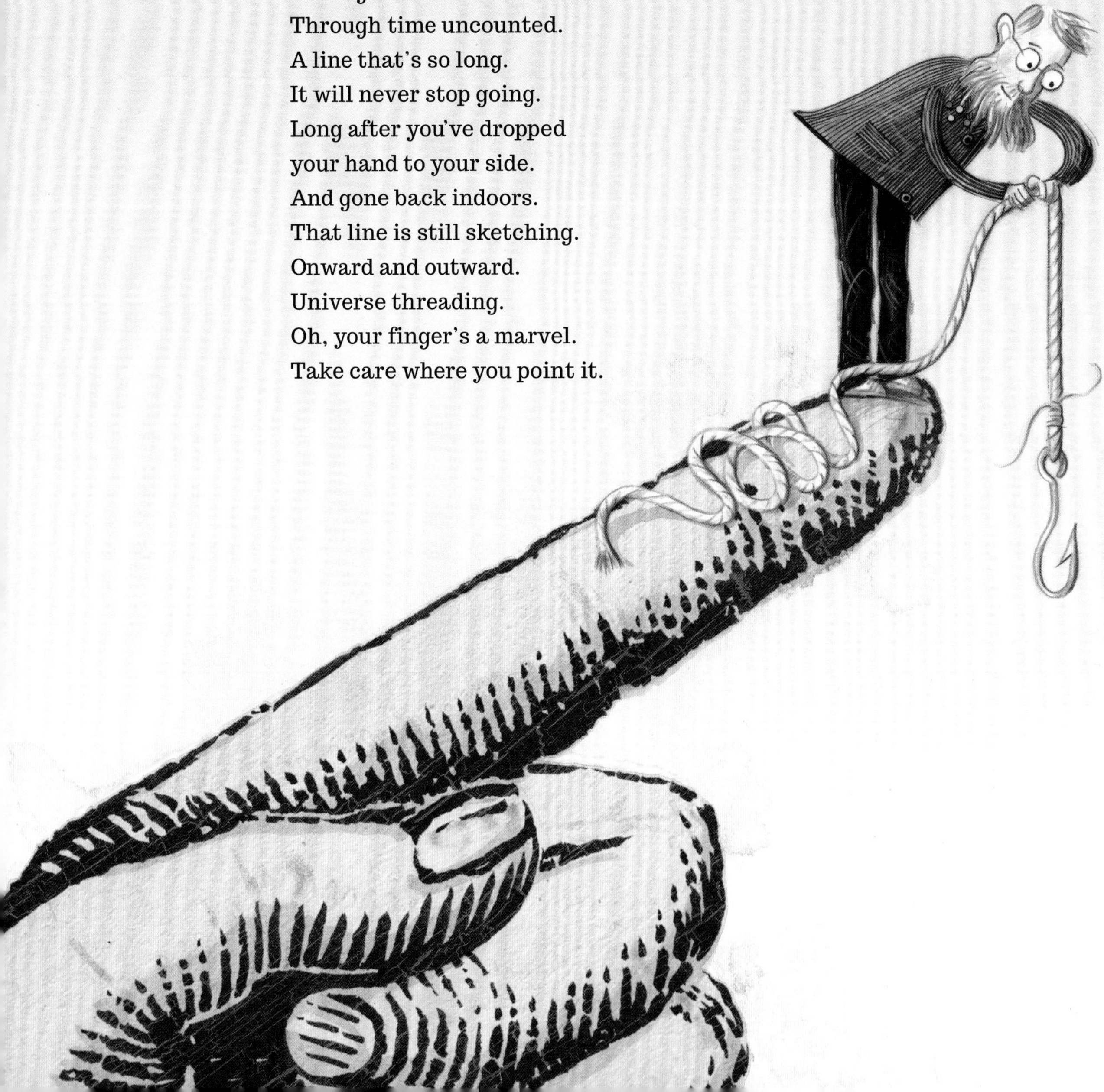

Winch

Back up
the pickup
truck.

Hook the hook
in the seat
of your soul.

Let the motor
run,
purring, winding,
and feel yourself
perked up,
picked up.

Each person's
particular pickup truck
is different—

a person,
a place,
a piece of music,
a smile,
a cuddle,
a hedgehog called Clive.

Finding it
can be tricky,
but so can calculating
equations
to guide a spaceship to Jupiter,
but someone did it.

So, fed up?
Find your pickup truck, pal,
and hook it up.

Perils of the Bouncy Castle

The merits are debatable
of a castle that's inflatable.

As defensive buildings go
a bouncy castle's just *so-so.*

From a distance it looks impressive,
but from closer up it's less. If

the enemy fires an arrow
your survival chances are narrow.

(And if your majesty wears a spiky crown:
don't bounce too high and don't fall down.)

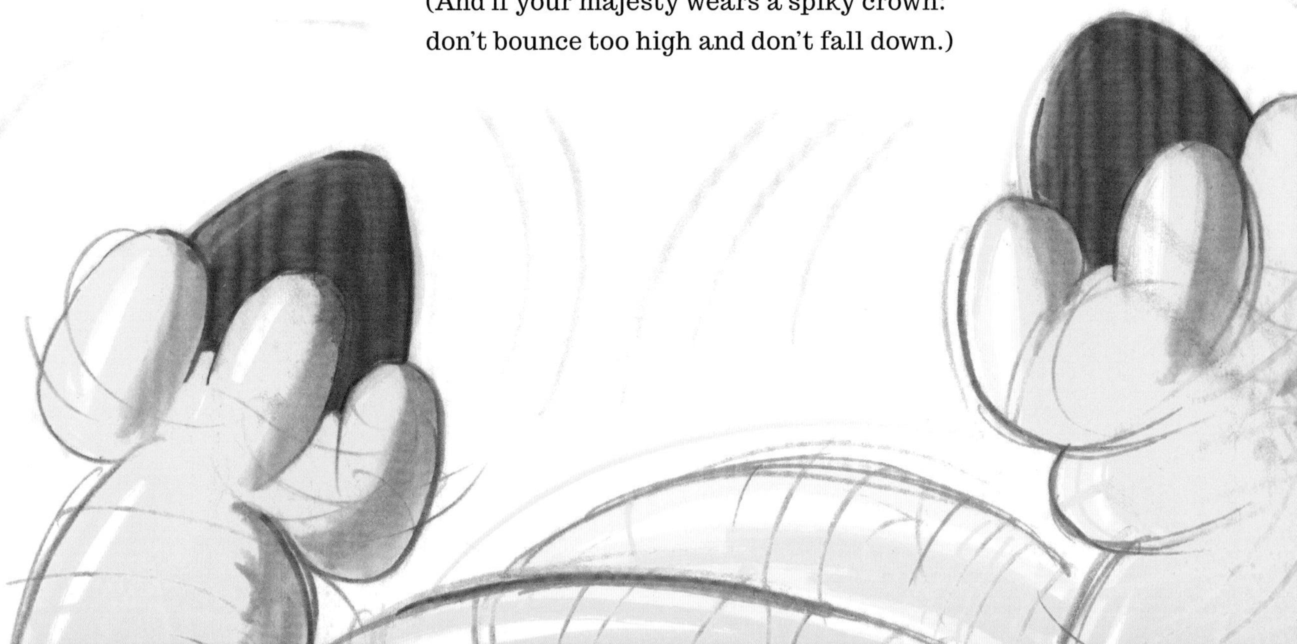

Missing

This poem is missing.
I've looked everywhere.

Under the sofa.
Over here, over there.

I can't seem to find it.
It's missing, it's true.

In place of that poem . . .
will this one do?

Some Final Further Notes for the Reader

Thank you for having read this book. We hope you've found it useful.

Let us leave you with a few final bits of free-floating advice, unattached to any poems, that you can cut out and keep for no extra charge.

Never be afraid.
Most laughter is a good thing.
Legs are useful for keeping your feet a sensible distance away from your nose.
You are not alone. We all feel like that, sometimes.
Love the people you have, or at least put up with them the best you can.
Say thank you every now and then.
Don't put your ear in a crocodile.

Final Notes for the Reader Wishing to Continue Their Adventure in Advice

Look over there, on the opposite page . . . It's your very own blank Advice-a-Tron 216.

For the Beginnings of your sentences, choose either words that set a time ("On Thursdays" or "Never") or a place ("In the supermarket" or "In the garden") or a certain set of circumstances ("When meeting the queen" or "If lost").

Your Middles should be a verb or doing word of some sort ("eat" or "squeeze" or "write a poem about").

And then your Endings should be nouns of some description ("kittens" or "a man called Greg" or "the queen").

Then you're ready to roll your dice and create your own not entirely useful advice.

Finally, instead of writing your words in the book in felt tip, why not photocopy the page with the machine on, and make loads of Advice-a-trons.

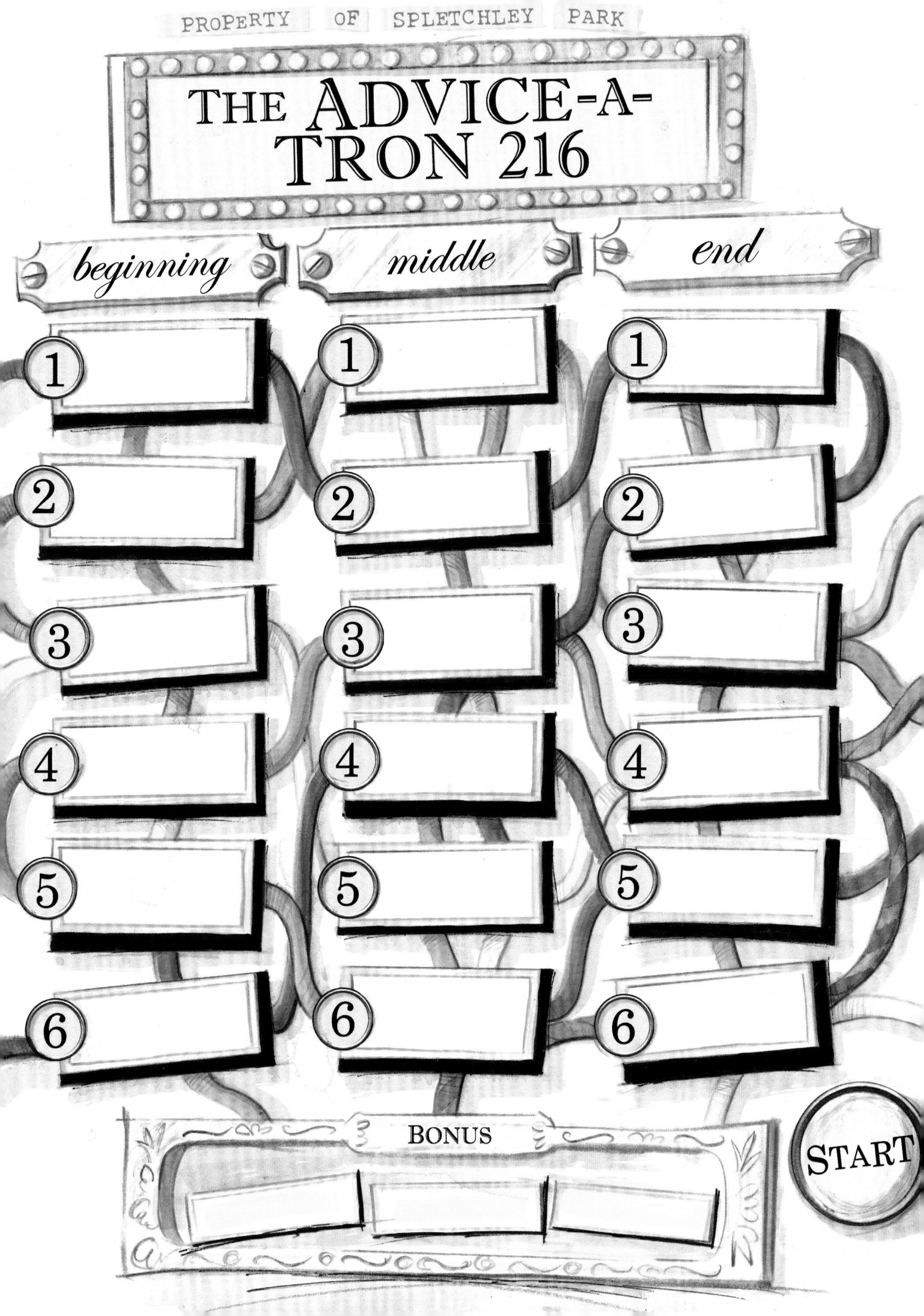
PROPERTY OF SPLETCHLEY PARK
THE ADVICE-A-TRON 216
beginning
middle
end
1
2
3
4
5
6
1
2
3
4
5
6
1
2
3
4
5
6
BONUS
START

Index of Advice, Examples, Morals, and Useful Lessons

A

Advice
examples of (not entirely) useful advice . . . 3–124
except 98

Advice-a-tron 216
what page the Advice-a-tron 216 is on . . . 65
what page the instructions for the Advice-a-tron 216 are on 64
where to find the means to construct your own Advice-a-tron 216 124–5

Aeroplane
how to attract an 12

Ambition
why other people's ambition can be bad for you . . 58–9

Anthill
how to get inside an 60

Ants
a terpsichorean use for 104

Arrows
obvious dangers involved with 120

B

Badges
good ideas of pictures and slogans to put on your . . . . vi–ix

Banana
how to identify a 18

Bath
how to be safe in a 58–9, 114

Beach

sea **Side**

Bear

how to check whether one is in your cornflakes or not . 3
number of them that Goldilocks encountered . . 3

Bee

what they need to visit in order to make honey . . 16

Belt

what makes a bad 74–5

Bin

how to make money using a 100

Birthday

why you shouldn't get too excited about your 91

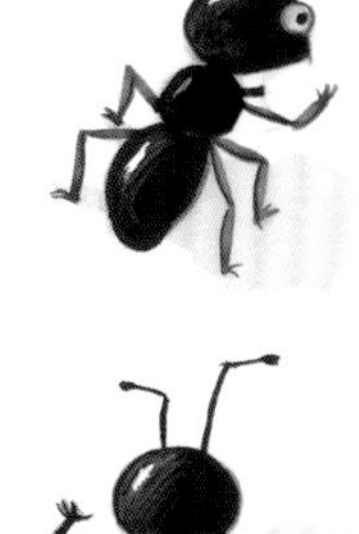

Biscuits

the worst sort 26–7

Blackbird

how to identify a 18

Blank space

a fine example of some 38–9
what to do with a 12

Boast

how to 7
what happens when you stop 109

Boat

fill with **Gravy**

Book

how to find out other books written by A. F. Harrold . ii
reasons to not eat a 31
the noise they make before being read . . . 102
what a book smells like . . . . *sniff this page*
where to find more . . . . *the library*
why they stick in the brain 72

Boomerang
why democracy is imperfect 34

Bouncy castle
basic safety tips 120

Breakfast
avoiding boredom in your 4
avoiding cabbages in your 9
dangers of wild animals in your 3
how to use it to avoid paying for lunch . . . 62

Bricks
the correct uses for 30

Broccoli
warning on the general dangers of 34

Broth
see **Cooks**

Bullies
how to deal with 68

Burger
how to not choke to death on a 19

Butler
what to do with your 108

Butterfly
how they scare off hungry things 17

Buttocks
a good place to put your 16

C

Cake
some examples of beautiful 16–17
what you will probably spill a bit of while making a 16

Camouflage
some examples of 17

Carpet
an example of something to not put on a . . . 73

Carrot
a good, non-eating, use for a . . . 47

Castle
basic defensive tips relating to a . . . 120

Cat
how to make one angry 77
how to make one happy 34
how to spot one in a restaurant 22
the noise they make when walking 102

Chair
a reason to place your buttocks on a . . . 16

Change the subject
how to . . . 106

Cheer up
how to help yourself to . . . 119

Cheese
what happens when you put it in a biscuit 26–7

Climate change
reasons to be angry about . . . 63

Clock
the noise one makes between ticking and tocking 102

Clouds
the noise they make when not ready to rain 102
things you should know about 96

Compliment
how to give a 112–13

Cooks
see **Broth**

Crisps
a variety of possible flavors, explored 32

Crown
basic safety instructions for wearing a . . . 120

D

Dairy

how to use a 73

Dancing

how to do so, like a poet 104

Dark

how to not be afraid of the 94

Diary

how to use a 73

Distraction

an example of a buttock-related 42

Dog

a beginner's guide to the 45

games to play with a 45, 50

what not to do with a living 51

Dolphin

there are no dolphins in this book, sorry . . *try other books*

Dreams

why they should be treasured, even when awake . . 72, 97

Droppings

under what circumstances you should and shouldn't eat 48

Duck

how to remove one from soup 10

how to use one to end a poem you don't otherwise know how to end 33

Dunking

general advice regarding the act of 24

Duvet

suggestion for making a really cold 34

Sometimes if you want something to exist you have to make it yourself.

E

Eagle
how to recognize an 76

Earlobe
how to recognize an 76

Ears
what not to put behind them 14

Earth
reasons to care about the 63

Egg
where they come from 15
what you can't make without cracking an 16

Elephant
how to recognize an 76
what to do with what comes out of an 47

Engagement ring
how to recognize an 76

Envelope
how to recognize an 76

Evening at the theater
how to recognize an 76

Exaggerate
how to do it and what happens when you stop . . 109

Exercise
how to get some 116

Exploring
how to do it without leaving your house . . . 72

ZOLA
BOURB

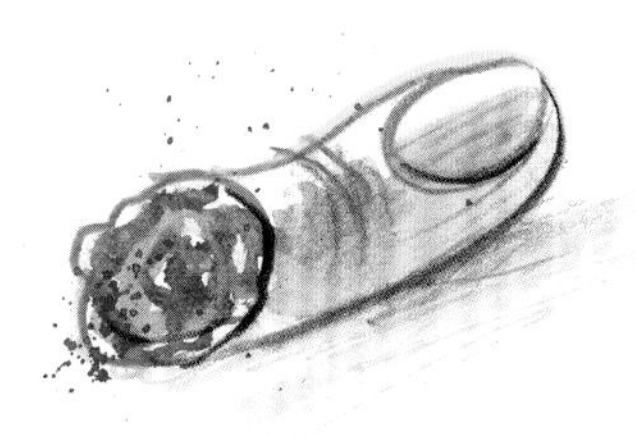

F

Farmer

general advice about being a 15

Feet

what they smell like . . . . . sniff your feet

why you shouldn't just waggle your 58–9

Finger

a most impressive use for a 118

Fire

how to put out a 114

Flour

how to disappoint a bee with a spelling mistake . not in this book

what you might make while spilling some 16

Flower

what you get when a bee has visited this spelling of flour . 16

Fortune telling

how to use a teabag for 28

Fox

general facts about the 52

Friends

how to identify ones to not invite to your house . . 24

G

Garden

fun activities to do in the 51

Geometric shapes

how to correctly name 70

Giant

good ways of avoiding being caught by a 57

why it's pointless trying to defend against a 57

Gloves
how to ruin a perfectly good pair of 50

Granny
finding the perfect "get well soon" gift for your 8
why you should never say "Yes" when she offers biscuits . 26–7

Grapes
how to get the juice out of 107

Gravy
see **Boat**
what not to do with 14

H

Hat
how to look like a 107
various tips relating to a 77
why they aren't a perfect disguise, despite what opera teaches you 86–7

Head
what happens when you put a bird's nest on your 77
what happens when you put a librarian on your 77
what happens when you put an angry cat on your 77
what happens when you put an octopus on your 77
what happens when you put some air on your 77
what you'll look like if you sit on someone's 107

Hedgehog
games to play with a 50
how to annoy a 50, 53, 107
how to be annoyed by a 50, 53, 107

Heights
how to stop being scared of 99

Holiday
how to avoid buying lunch while on 62

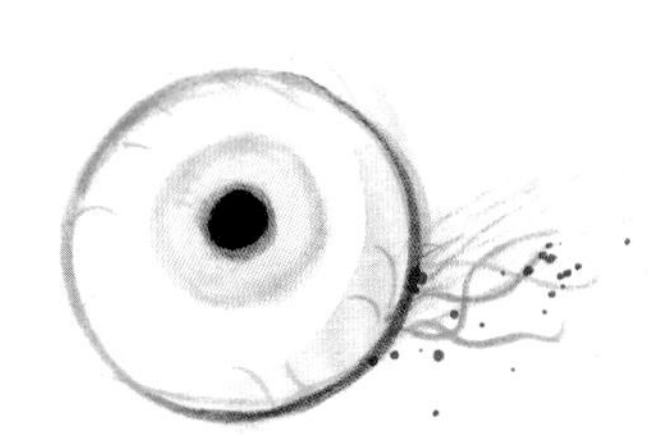

Honey
fictional bear most likely to be caught with a pot of . . . . . . Pooh
what you need to make 16

Horner, Jack
how to recognize 16

I

Idea
how to have one every day 73
where to find an 98

J

Jelly
general advice about 33
where there might be some . . . . the kitchen

Juggle
essential advice for learning how to 42

Jumper
how to put on a 116

Jungle
things you might find in a 117

K

Kilt
how to not answer the eternal mystery of the 55

Kissing
life-saving advice regarding 43

Koala
the best metaphor for life is the 55

L

Lamp posts
where they come from 61

Legs
how to stop people from seeing your 17
what might break your 16
see also **Trousers**; *don't see* **Legs**

Lies
how to answer difficult questions using 98

Life
how to make it less boring 97

Lion
how to avoid being eaten by a 99

List
why you should think carefully before making a 87

Local
how to tell if something is 63

Lunch
how to use breakfast to avoid paying for 62

Lunch box
an explanation of the noises coming from your 18
why you shouldn't mix one up with a pencil case . . 71

M

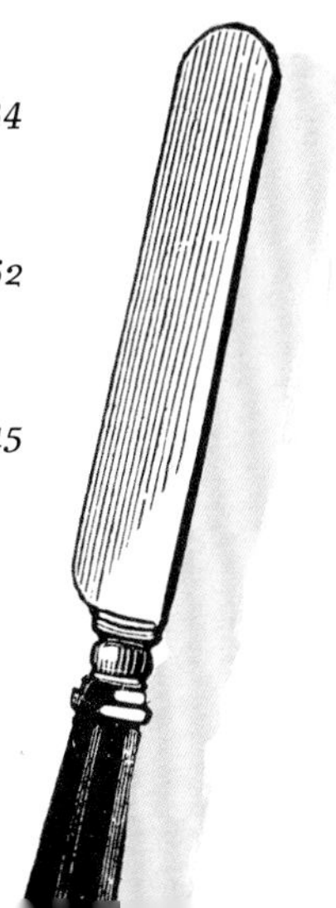

Mice
how to make them unhappy 34

Migration
which animals go on a 62

Milk
where it comes from 15

Mistakes

how to make them and still maintain your dignity . . 117

Money

how to get lots of 100

Monkeys

why you should ignore 42

Moon

the noise it makes when in the sky . . . 102

what it looks like in the afternoon . . . 80

Moose

how to make into a burger, safely 19

Morning

how to wake up on time in the 107

what meal to have first thing in the 3, 4, 7

Mother

how to not upset your 51

how to say "Thank you" or "I love you" to your 8

how to upset your 51

when you shouldn't listen to your 14

Mustache

how to impersonate someone with a 12

N

Night

the noise it makes when falling 102

Nighttime noises

how to not be afraid of 94

Non sequitur

an example of how to use one to end a poem . . 33

O

Oblong
what shape an oblong is not 70

Old joke
how to put a new twist on an 78–9

Omelette
do not see **Shakespeare***: that's "Hamlet" you're thinking of*
what you have to crack in order to make an 16

Onion
a good use for a 68
how to cry when you're not sad . . . . *sniff one*

Opera
how to get your own way by singing 103

P

Paradox
how to experience a 91

Parrot
a beginner's guide to the 45
don't listen to the words the parrot says, sometimes they swear 5, 44

Pegs
a good use for 16

Pencil
an example of the incorrect use of a 71

Pencil case
why you shouldn't muddle one up with a lunch box . . 71

People
how to discover which people this book's dedicated to . v
how to see people . . . . *look out your window*

Pet
advice on choosing a 46–7
what not to do with a 50

Picnic
how to not let tigers ruin your 20
how to really enjoy a . . . 20
scientific uses of a . . . 60

Pie
possible fillings for a . . . 16
see also Banana, Blackbird, Crisps, Duck, Mice, Onion, People, Pig, *etc.*

Pig
why you shouldn't get too close to a really fat one 86–7

Plum
where it belongs 16

Poem
one that's not in the book 121

Poetry
how to learn what poems are in this book and on which pages vi–ix
how to use it for purposes of revenge 105
what the point of it is 34

Pollution
reasons to be angry about . . . 63

Porcupine
reasons to not eat a . . . 31
whether you should keep one in your bra 34

Potter, Harry
number of novels in the original series, by J. K. Rowling 7

Pudding
the correct uses for . . . 30–1

Q

Quiet
what a quiet poem sounds like 79

R

Rabbit
what you should and shouldn't do if you are a . . . 48
why you shouldn't poke a . . . 49

Rain
how to avoid getting wet in the . . . 115

Rainbow
one of the key ingredients in making a . . . 16

Raisin
why you should look closely before eating a . . . 48

Reading (not the town in Berkshire)
why it's a good thing 72

Reading (the town in Berkshire)
why it's a good thing *go there and ask*

Rectangle
another word for 70

Restaurants
signs to watch out for, in order to avoid a bad one 22

Rhinoceros
what to do with what comes out of a . . . 47

Rich people
how to get money out of . . . 100

Ring
an example of gemstones you might use to decorate a . . . 30

Road
how to be safe when crossing the . . . 92

Rock
correct safety procedures for handling . . . 29
some examples of beautiful . . . 16–17

Rock cake
how they defend themselves 17
some examples of beautiful . . . 16–17

Roll
which ones not to eat 29

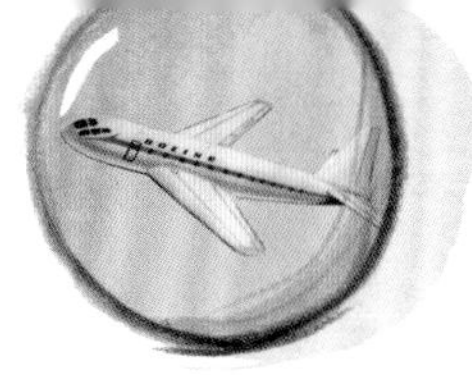

S

Sailor
sea **Legs**

Sand
how much it takes to spoil a sandwich . . . *20*

Sausage
advice on what to not make one from . . . *34*
multiple uses for a *12*

Sausage roll
an example of an incorrect use for a *71*

Scientific curiosity
an example of *60*

Secrets
the noise they make when no one spills them . . *102*

Shakespeare
year of birth *1564*
year of death *1616*
year of first eating a tomato . . . . *unknown*

Shark
how to attract a *12*

Sheep
how to set loose the *107*

Shiplofting
why you shouldn't go *110*

Shoplifting
why you shouldn't go *110*

Shower
the upside of a *16*

Shy
how to spot if a poem is *79*

Silence
how to spot a good *102*

Simile
how to use them to great effect 106

Singing
the worst sort of 103

Sister
cruel things they can do to you 105
cruel things to do to your 34
how to get rid of an annoying 49

Skiing trip
the ingredients for a successful 16

Snake
what to do if you are a 43
why you shouldn't use one to hold your trousers up . . 74–5

Socks
things to not do to 34

Soup
how to remove a duck from 10
how to upset a cat with 11
your favorite flavor of . . . . . . *how should I know?*

Spaghetti
why you shouldn't use it to hold your trousers up . . 75

Spelling
why it's not to be taken seriously 85

Spider
how to avoid being eaten by a 58–9
how to avoid seeing a 99

Spoon
how many it takes to spoil soup 20

Square
what does a square look like? 70

Stick
what might happen if you throw a 45

String
how to spot if it's tangled 93

T

Teabag
things to do with a 28

Teacher
finding the perfect "Sorry you're leaving" gift for your 8
how to not upset your 99

Things
that are in this book *i–148*
that aren't in this book . . . . *everywhere else*

Things to say
nice ones 112–13

Thumb
what to do with a 16

Tiger
how many it takes to spoil a picnic . . . 20
how to see that Mini can draw a brilliant 21
how to spot a hiding 3, 6

Toast
something you can do with 7

Trousers
an example of a good material from which to make 30
see also **Legs**

U

Umbrella
general tips for use of an 115

Universe
how to recognize your place in the 118

V

Vertigo
how to cope with 99

W

Waiter
how to upset a 10

Washing line
what looks good on a 16

Wednesday
how it feels 83

Window
a good use for a 108

Wood
the correct uses for 30

Worm
why you shouldn't use one to hold your trousers up . 74–5

Wrist
what not to dab on your 14

Z

Zombie
how to help a 78
this is the end of the book, thank you for reading it . 148

Acknowledgments

Some of these poems were first published elsewhere, sometimes in slightly different forms:

"Some Home Truths" and "Umbrella Poem" were first published in *Scoop* magazine (2017)

"Parrots Are Not to be Confused with Dogs," "Playing with Pets," "How to Avoid a Giant Who Has Escaped from a Nearby Fairy Tale," "Inside the Anthill," and "Bath Poem" were first published in *I Eat Squirrels* (Quirkstandard's Alternative, 2009; illustrated by A. F. Harrold)

"The Perils of Breakfast," "The New Farmer Learns," "Burger Tips," "Smaller Ones Are Better," "Burying the Dog," "The Ambitious Spider," "In the Dark," and "Dreamless" were first published in *Things You Find in a Poet's Beard* (Burning Eye Books, 2015; illustrated by Chris Riddell)

A. F. Harrold is the author of *The Afterwards*; *The Imaginary*, which was a *Kirkus Reviews* Best Middle Grade Book; and *The Song from Somewhere Else*, which received four starred reviews and was both a *School Library Journal* and *Wall Street Journal* Best Book; as well as an English poet who writes and performs for adults and children. He is the owner of many books, a handful of hats, and one beard. He spends his spare time showing off on stage, at schools, and at home, and his non-spare time sitting around stroking his beard and writing things down. He lives in Reading, England, with a stand-up comedian and two cats.

www.afharroldkids.com

Mini Grey studied sequential design at Brighton University before launching her first picture book, *Egg Drop*, in 2002. Trained in puppet making, set design, welding, and carpentry, Mini's style has an unconventional flare and instantly recognizable quirkiness. Mini has now published thirteen picture books. Among numerous nominations and prizes, Mini has won the CILIP Kate Greenaway Medal for *The Adventures of the Dish and the Spoon*.

BUM